Anonymous

The Saint Nicholas Christmas Book

Vol. 1

Anonymous

The Saint Nicholas Christmas Book
Vol. 1

ISBN/EAN: 9783337378981

Printed in Europe, USA, Canada, Australia, Japan

Cover: Foto ©Andreas Hilbeck / pixelio.de

More available books at **www.hansebooks.com**

The St. Nicholas Christmas Book

Merry Christmas!

New York: The Century Co.

1901

THE DE VINNE PRESS.

Contents

The St. Nicholas Christmas Book

The St. Nicholas Christmas Book

DECEMBER

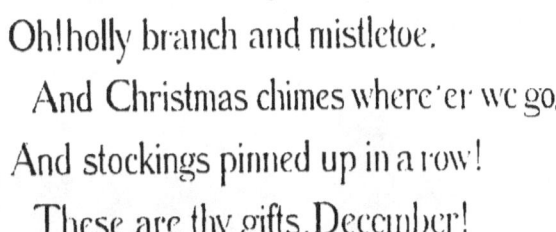

I

Oh! holly branch and mistletoe.
　And Christmas chimes where'er we go,
And stockings pinned up in a row!
　These are thy gifts, December!

And if the year has made thee old,
And silvered all thy locks of gold,
Thy heart has never been a-cold
Or known a fading ember.

The whole world is a Christmas tree,
And stars its many candles be.
Oh! sing a carol joyfully
The year's great feast in keeping!

For, once, on a December night
An angel held a candle bright,
And led three wise men by its light
To where a child was sleeping.

Harriet F. Blodgett.

President for One Hour

BY FRED P. FOX

T was just eight o'clock as the passenger-train pulled out of the Wayville station on the morning of December 24, 1891. The train was heavily laden with merry people either bound for their Eastern homes, or gay holiday shoppers going to the city to purchase the last supply of presents that were to make the coming day the happiest of the year.

The mail-car and express-cars were laden to overflowing with many queer-shaped packages, and even the spaces in the vestibules between the cars had to be utilized for " through " pouches and packages, so great was the jam of Christmas presents.

If it was a jolly crowd that left the little station, it was not an unhappy one that remained. The fog had so settled down upon and around everything that the little lamp in the telegraph and ticket office shed but a feeble light upon the persons seated around the stove. There is always a crowd in a country station at train-time, and in spite of the rules a few privileged persons always find their way into the office.

Merrily the telegraph instrument ticked away, sending its messages of hope or grief across a continent. As he sat beside the instrument, Fred Clarke, the operator, once in a while gave out a bit of electric gossip to the entertained listeners. " No. 13 is five minutes late at Bloss," he remarked. Then he smiled as he said, " The general manager has just left High Ridge on his 'special,' coming west. He must have a jolly party with him, for he has ordered fourteen dinners at Glenmore to be ready when he arrives there. His car will pass here at 9: 10."

" What engine 's pulling the ' special '? " asked Bob Ford, one of the listeners.

" No. 39."

" That 's father's old engine," spoke up Tom Martin, a dark-eyed, dark-haired boy of fifteen years, who had been gazing intently into the fire.

4

"He used to run her on all the specials, until he was killed in the accident at Oak Bridge two years ago."

"Right you are, lad," said Bob Ford; "and it's many the time I fired for him on old 39. He was as brave and as true a man as ever pulled a lever. You used to ride with us often, too — did n't you, Tom?"

"Yes; until one day the general manager saw me sitting in the cab, and issued an order that after that day no one but regular employees in the discharge of their duty should ride upon the engines. I have never been on an engine since; but I learned a great deal about them — did n't I, Bob?"

"Yes, you did, Tom; and, for a boy, you can do as much about an engine as any youngster I know. I would rather have you around than many a fellow I know who's now running an engine. What are you doing now?"

"Since father's death I do whatever I can to help support my mother, and I find enough to keep me out of mischief. I attend night-school, and during the day I carry the mail between the depot and town, carry dinners and lunches for the men, sell papers, and deliver messages. Besides, I am Fred's pupil, and have learned telegraphy."

"Are you making a living at all these odd jobs?"

"Yes, I am; but of course I can't make what father made; and we are trying to pay off the mortgage on the house. I do wish, though, I could do better. Here it is Christmas-time, and I have been saving money for three months — yes, six — in order to buy mother a nice warm cloak; but when I came to price them I found that the five dollars and a half I had saved would not get anything at all like what I wanted. It would take three dollars more, at least. How I would like to have surprised my dear old mother! But then, no matter; I can get her something else that's nice, and we will have a merry Christmas, anyway."

"You say you can telegraph," said Bob, after a moment; "what are the wires saying now?"

"The operator at High Ridge is asking whether No. 14 left here on time. What's that?" he continued excitedly. "Keep still! Rockville is saying, 'Freight-train — No. 37 — broke into three sections — at Cantwell. Engineer — thinking there was one break and that rear section was under control — started back to couple on. Dense fog — met middle section coming at full speed — engineer and fireman thrown from engine. Engine and three cars running east down-grade at full speed.' That's terrible!" he said. "But listen — 'Middle section, one mile behind, just passed — ten loaded stock-cars — Jack Flynn clinging to rear car. Must stop train if you can. If 14 has not yet left, switch her to west-bound track or she'll be lost.'" Then the instrument stopped ticking.

"Is that right, Fred?" Bob asked the operator, as soon as he found his breath; "or has Tom been joking with us?"

"It's all true!"answered Fred. "That's just what's happened! What shall we do? What *can* we do?"

There was no answer to this appeal. The blanched faces of the listeners showed that all understood the horror of the situation.

No. 14, the passenger-train that had just left, was bowling leisurely along at thirty miles an hour, crowded with passengers. Behind, and coming with resistless force, was a runaway engine and three cars, running sixty miles an hour, and behind that train was the heavy broken section, ten loaded stock-cars, coming nearly as fast.

There seemed to be no hope for the doomed passengers, since on the west-bound track the general manager's through express was approaching. To attempt to switch the runaway engine or section would be likely to tear up the track, and the chances were that the loss of life would be just as great, if not greater, than to let the engine speed on its way. No wonder the men turned pale as they understood the situation of affairs. No wonder that the stoutest hearts stood still. For, as they reflected, horror seemed to pile on horror.

Then out of the gloom there came a steady voice: it seemed filled with an inspiration. It was an opportunity for the genius of a true "railroad man"; and the man, or rather boy, was there, ready to prove his capacity.

The boy Tom spoke up: "All of you men get out and oil the track — pour on oil, put on grease, smear it with tallow, or anything! That will keep back the engine a little — perhaps enough. After the engine has passed, keep on with the work. Remember we've got to save Flynn's life — yes, and save the cattle, too."

The men at once ran out of the depot, Fred and Bob leading.

"Now, I must save No. 14!" said Tom to himself. "I'll have to keep the west-bound track clear, and then switch No. 14 on to it at Lewistown."

With steady fingers he grasped the telegraph key, and this message flew along the wire:

Operator, Mount Vernon: Flag special train of general manager, and tell him to wait for orders. T. M.

Back came the inquiry, in a moment, from the Mount Vernon office:

"THE MEN HAD OILED THE TRACK THOROUGHLY FOR SEVERAL HUNDRED YARDS."

T. M., Wayville: Who has right to stop special? Track has been cleared for the general manager's train. By whose orders shall I tell him he has been flagged?

It was no time to stick at trifles or to make explanations, so Tom flashed back the answer:

By orders of president of the U. S. R. R., per T. M.

"O. K.," answered Mount Vernon, as a sign that the order was understood and would be obeyed.

"Now, to get 14 switched from the east- to the west-bound track! There is just a chance." Again he touched the key.

Operator, Lewistown: Turn cross-over switch at your station; transfer passenger-train No. 14 from east- to west-bound track, and hold her there until released. T. M.

Then the key ticked in reply:

T. M., Wayville: Track has been cleared for special of general manager. His train approaching from east with regular orders giving right of way. Make your order more definite, and give authority.

As before, Tom was ready, and answered:

Operator, Lewistown: President of U. S. R. R. Co. does not have to show authority. Carry out the orders at once. Important. T. M.

" O. K.," ticked back the reply.

" Now," said Tom to himself, "if I can only delay the engine until 14 gets across on the other track, everything will be all right. The poor horses and cattle will have to take their chances. Let 's see— 14 has been gone fifteen minutes ; she is due at Lewistown in thirty minutes. The runaway engine will be here in about five minutes, unless her speed is reduced; the passenger-train will be overtaken about five miles this side of Lewistown. There is only one hope now. I must risk it."

"WITH STEADY FINGERS HE GRASPED THE TELEGRAPH KEY."

Just then the ticket-agent, hearing the men hurrying about, had come down-stairs and asked the trouble. As briefly as he could, Tom told him the situation, and then said: " Mr. Lenox, I 'm going to climb into the runaway engine, if it 's a possible thing, and check her up. I 've five dollars or so here. Take it and, if I 'm hurt, give it to my mother. Tell her I was going to get her a Christmas present, and tell her I know that she would tell me to do just what I 'm going to do. God bless her! If I come out all right — and there is a chance — don't ever let her know what I did. Promise, quick!"

" Don't think of such a thing, Tom," pleaded the agent. " Why, it 's suicide! If you can slow down the engine, when you get aboard, the rear section will run into you and crush you. If you can't, you are sure to run into the passenger-train and die in the collision. In this fog, even if you get control of the engine,—and I doubt if you can,—you cannot tell what second you will be upon the passenger-train, or what second the other section will be upon you. You are the only support of your mother. Just as likely as not, you will be killed in your attempt to get on the engine. No one ever got on an engine going as fast as this one is; why, to try it is worse than suicide! Then, the engine might blow up. You *must* not attempt it!"

"It 's all very true, Mr. Lenox; but it 's better to try, even if I fail, when so many lives will be lost unless an effort is made to save them. I am going to do all I can, and as for mother — why, God bless her! Good-by. I must get out on the platform to be ready."

"Good-by, and Heaven help you, Tom," replied Mr. Lenox.

Before going out, Tom took off his well-worn overcoat and jacket, tightened up his belt, and prepared to run the race of his life. He then went out to the platform and found that the men had oiled the track thoroughly for several hundred yards. He did not dare tell them of his purpose for fear that they would stop him; but he said to Bob: "After the engine passes, get all the men you can at work — more are coming every minute; put on all the oil you can, and tallow, but be careful to see that there is nothing to make the cars jump the track, for that will kill all the cattle and horses, and perhaps poor Jack Flynn! He was seen clinging to the last car at Rockville. But he dared not climb up or jump off, it seems, on account of the speed of the train. There she comes now—I can hear her. I 'll run up to the other end of the platform to meet her."

The engine could be heard thundering down the track long before she could be seen coming through the fog. Tom was at the far end of the depot, where the men had first begun to apply the oil and grease; and, as they had worked back, he was in a position to get all the benefit of the loss of speed in consequence. The men flew back from the track. When the engine struck the oiled rails she trembled, and her wheels slipped rather than revolved along the track. The momentum was so great that at first the speed was scarcely affected; but as successive sections of track were passed, there began to be quite a marked reduction in speed. Tom noticed this with joy.

The engine was coming rapidly toward him. He turned and ran along the platform in the same direction as the engine, at a speed that would have carried him fifty yards in about six seconds. The engine gained on him, and, just as the step was passing, he reached up, grasped the handles, and swung himself up on the step. He rested there for a few seconds, and then climbed slowly up into the cab. His face was as white as the card on the steam-gauge, and, in spite of the cold wind that blew upon him, he was dripping with perspiration.

Tom glanced up at the gauge, and saw that the supply of steam was being rapidly exhausted, and, to his horror, he understood that the engine was running by its own inertia down the steep grade. He closed the throttle, set the lever one notch on the reverse side, and then tried the air-brake. It worked in a feeble way, but checked the engine a trifle. He found that in order to gain control of the engine he must get up more steam, and get the air-pump running.

Tom slowly crept along the flying engine over the tender, and was pleased to find that there was plenty of water in the tank. Being as strong a young fellow of fifteen years as one often sees, he had no trouble in getting up a brisk fire. He then went back to the engine, and was gratified to see the steam was rapidly coming up. There was no thought of fear in the brave boy, but he did not forget that he was "between two fires." He must keep his own engine from running into the passenger-train, and he must keep ahead and out of the way of the runaway section. Anxiously he peered out into the fog; but he could see nothing of the train he was pursuing, and could hear nothing of the train that was pursuing him. On sped the flying steed of steel, and still the pointer on the steam-gauge moved slowly upward. Twenty pounds more pressure, and he felt that he would have complete control of the engine. He was using but little steam now — only enough to try the air-pump now and then. In a few moments he moved back the lever another notch toward the reverse, and cautiously pulled out the throttle a little. The effect was good, and he knew that he was gaining control of the engine; but how she flew along over culvert, bridge, and trestle, like a thing of life on a wild holiday!

Out came the throttle a little farther, and back went the lever another notch. The engine was running slower. "By reversing her and putting on the 'emergency air,'" Tom said to himself, "I can now stop her in three or four lengths. It would be a bad thing to do, but I'll do it if I have to." He looked up at the clock. "In five minutes more No. 14 will have passed to the other track and the switch will be closed. I'll slow up a bit"; and so he did.

The engine promptly responded, and settled down to a forty-mile gait. Tom, with his head far out of the window, with one hand on the throttle and the other on the air-lever, tried to pierce the mist with those bright dark eyes, but in vain. Boom! and a torpedo exploded under the wheels.

"No. 14 has stopped — to switch!" said Tom. Boom! boom! Again came the warning torpedoes. "'Run slowly, with the engine under full control'; that 's what those mean." Suddenly Tom's attention was called to a thundering sound from the rear.

"It 's the broken section coming like a whirlwind. Now I 'm in for it. If she will hold off for two minutes I 'll be all right." Tom threw the lever full ahead, and opened the throttle; the engine seemed to leap forward. In a minute more he caught just a glimpse of the rear lights on the passenger-train, and knew that a minute later he would be upon her. Nearer came

"HE GRASPED THE HANDLES AND SWUNG HIMSELF UP ON THE STEP."

the thundering roar behind him, and he dared not look back. The light in front swerved to the left. Would the switch be closed in time for him to keep ahead of the pursuing section? was the question which flew through his brain. His engine was at the switch, and it had just been replaced! "Thank God for that!" was the brief prayer he murmured. "The passenger-train is safe, if my orders have been carried out. Now to save myself, and the cattle behind me. It 's a race for life, and I ought to win!"

A tangent[1] of twelve miles lay straight before him, with a gently descending grade, then a mile level, and then a four-mile up-grade into Mount Vernon. Once more he crept down into the tender, opened wide the fur-

1 A section of track without a curve.

nace doors, raked the fire, and threw in the coal evenly over every part of the great fire-box. He left the ash-pit door open for better draft, and then climbed upon the coal to see if he could distinguish his relentless pursuer. The light had begun to dispel the fog, and three hundred feet away he could see the on-coming train. "It will take all the speed she's got," he thought, and leaving the tender he crept back into the cab.

He opened the throttle wide, pushing the lever over forward as far as it would go. The steam kept up, and the only thing to fear was that the

"HE OPENED WIDE THE FURNACE DOORS AND THREW IN THE COAL."

axle-boxes would get heated on account of the frightful speed of the engine; but then he reflected that the pace would tell on the freight-axles even more, since they were not geared to so high a speed as were those of the locomotive.

The engine was now going at the rate of a mile a minute, or faster. More coal was necessary, and he resolved to leave the window and stand by the furnace. In ten minutes the level was struck, and the pursuer had gained two hundred feet, on account of its greater weight; a minute later the up-grade was reached. More coal was needed, and the shovel was kept busy feeding the fiery mouth whose tongues of flame seemed never to be satisfied. As the engine began the ascent of the up-grade, the freight section was only fifty feet away. After a mile on the grade, the locomotive pulled slowly away from the freight. Then Tom closed the ash-pit door, went back to the window, closed the throttle a little, tried the air-brakes, and three minutes later pulled into the depot at Mount Vernon, and came to a stop. He looked out of the window, perched high in air, and said to the operator: "Just wire Wayville that engine 303 has arrived here safely, and that Tom's all right."

The crowd of people who were on the platform surrounding the general manager's special car looked with amazement on the young engineer seated in the cab of the smoking engine. The general manager himself was not pleased at the sight, nor at the "unaccountable delay caused by some drunken operator," as he thought, who had imagined that he was the president of the road. He had not yielded with the best grace to the order stopping his train, and would not have heeded it but for the information that the same person had ordered the east-bound passenger-train over to the west-bound track, and his order had been obeyed, thus blocking the way. This passenger-train might now pull in at any minute. The operator could not get any reply from Wayville, to find out about the order.

"Well, young man," said the manager, "what are you doing up in that engine? Don't you know it's against orders? Where are the engineer and fireman? It makes no difference — they are discharged. Get down out of there! Where did you steal the engine?"

Tom could say nothing, but he did not move.

"Be lively there," continued the manager, in a rage. "Officer, arrest that boy for stealing the engine!"

"Grandpa, give him a chance to explain," said a young girl who stood near the angry official. "He does n't look as if he had stolen anything," she continued.

"I'll attend to him, Mary. He will have a chance to explain in court!"

"Please don't have him arrested," pleaded the young girl — and she seemed to be the only one who dared address her grandfather.

"My dear child, you don't understand these matters. Officer, get that fellow out of there. The engine looks as if it had been badly used."

The officer climbed up into the cab, and roughly shook Tom by the shoulder. Tom seemed dazed. What a fate, after all he had braved and done — to be received, instead of with thanks and praise, with threats of arrest and imprisonment!

"Come, get out of here — lively," said the officious policeman, anxious to show his authority before so high an official as the general manager of the U. S. R. R. Co. "You look to me like a pretty tough customer."

This roused Tom's ire.

" Don't touch me, please ; I 'll get down myself. I want to say just a word to Mr. Holmes." He walked up to that official and said : " I did not steal your engine, and — "

" I don't care to hear any talk," said the manager.

" I don't care to talk, either," said Tom, " but you 'd better send the engine back to the grade, and see what 's become of Jack Flynn. He was clinging to the rear car of a runaway section of train No. 37."

" What do you say ? — the train broken in two ? Where did it happen ? " asked Mr. Holmes, all interest at once.

" At Cantwell ; the train broke in two places, coming down the grade. The engine was struck by the flying center-section, hurling the engine crew off, and starting the engine the other way. I climbed on the runaway engine at Wayville, and brought her here. The rest of the train is back about two miles — unless she has run back down to the level."

" That 's a pretty story. How did you pass No. 14 ? " asked the manager, sternly, after thinking a moment.

" She was switched to the west-bound track at Lewistown," answered Tom.

" Tell the engineer and fireman on 39 to get up in this engine and run her back," said the manager to the conductor. " Officer, you bring the boy along, and I 'll go with you. If his story is true, he can go ; but if not, it will be all the harder for him."

The trainmen soon had the engine oiled up, finding it was none the worse for its fast run and that Tom had left everything in shipshape order. After backing down about two miles, a man was seen limping up the track. As the engine came nearer, Tom cried out : " It 's Jack Flynn — he 's all right ! "

Sure enough it was Flynn, but he was picked up more dead than alive. No one had ever taken, or perhaps will ever take, a ride like his. Briefly he told the story of the breaking of the train into three parts — an unheard-of thing, almost. He had been on the center-section, alone ; he had tried to apply the brakes, but the section he was on collided with the first section. He was thrown down on the top of a car, but had retained his senses enough to cling on. Then he had attempted to climb down on the last car, and drop off ; but the speed had been so great that he knew the fall would be fatal, and so he had clung to the rear car, expecting death at any moment. But the train came to an up-grade, and speed had been so reduced that he managed to climb up and set two of the brakes, but then he had to stop. The train gained in speed as it passed the down-grade, and he was glad to climb back again to his old place at the rear of the last car. Next the brakes had parted, and it seemed as if he were rushing to swift destruction. At last, the up-grade being reached, the cars lost speed; he could then have stepped off, but he resolved to stay on until the train stopped, because it was his duty. Just before the cars started to run back to the level, he had dragged a tie across the track and held the section.

"You can 'lay off' until New Year's day," said Mr. Holmes, after Flynn had finished his story. The engine had by this time stopped in front of the section of the stock-train. The cars were coupled on, and a few minutes later the whole train pulled into the depot at Mount Vernon.

The officer by this time had concluded not to put the handcuffs on Tom.

"Officer, you can let that boy go," gruffly ordered Mr. Holmes. "Who are you?" he asked Tom.

"I am Thomas Martin's son," he answered; "he used to run the engine of your special — 39."

"I thought I had seen you before. Go into my car and get warm. I see you have neither coat nor overcoat on, and this is a pretty cold day. Mary, get my overcoat and put it on that boy as soon as you can, and see that he gets a warm place; he is nearly frozen."

Tom was a little abashed as he walked into the magnificent private car of the general manager, escorted by that official's granddaughter. But he was soon at ease, and warmly wrapped in a big ulster.

Mr. Holmes went into the telegraph office, and directed that the passenger-train held at Lewistown should be switched back to its own track and started on its way.

He asked the operator at Wayville who had sent from that office the messages stopping his train, and by whose orders. No one at Wayville was in the office when the despatches were sent, and no copy of the messages could be found. The operator had been greasing the track, and had supposed Tom was similarly employed, as on account of the fog he could not tell the men apart.

"That's very strange," muttered Mr. Holmes, as he entered his car and signaled the engineer to go ahead. He was an honest, high-principled man, quick in his methods — the first to see a wrong, the first to right it. He was stern in all his dealings with his men, but he was also just, and they all respected him. He came back to where Tom was seated and said: "Well, young man, how are you coming on, and where do you want to get off?"

"I'm all right, and I want to get off at Wayville. The mail must be at the station, and I have to take it over to town."

"George," said Mr. Holmes to his son, who was the train-master of the road, "do you happen to remember where the president is to-day?"

"IT'S A RACE FOR LIFE, AND I OUGHT TO WIN."

" I think he is in New York."

" Well, I wonder who sent these messages?" said Mr. Holmes, handing them over to his son.

Tom flushed, but said nothing.

" They were sent from Wayville, by some man who must have had the running of the trains at his fingers' ends. A train-despatcher could have done no better. I don't know of any man at Wayville who could do it. Do you, Tom?" asked the train-master.

" Well, I don't think it was very much of a thing, only a fellow had to think pretty quick."

" Did *you* do it?" asked the general manager, suddenly.

" Yes, sir, I did."

" You sent the messages?"

" Yes, sir."

" Are you — besides being a fireman and an engineer — a train-despatcher and operator?"

" And president for an hour," chimed in Mary.

" Yes, sir; I plead guilty to all. But I was only acting president," said Tom.

" How dared you do such a thing?" asked Mr. Holmes.

" I dared do anything that would save human life. If some one had not dared, what would have happened? There was but one thing to do, and I did the best I could."

" You are not working for the company?"

" No, sir."

" Would you like to be?"

" Yes, sir."

" George, you see that Tom Martin is put on the rolls at fifty dollars a month, as messenger in the general manager's office. His salary began on December 1st, and he reports for duty on January 2d."

" Thank you, sir," said Tom, heartily.

WHEN the train pulled in at Wayville, there was a large crowd at the depot; and Tom was greeted with cheers as he stepped from the private car. He immediately threw the mail-pouches into the hand-cart that was standing near, and, without saying a word, started to fulfil his duty. Duty was first with him.

The general manager and his guests got off the train, and, mingling with the crowd, soon learned all that Tom had done in saving the train. They also learned, as they had already guessed, that he was brave, honest, and generous.

2

The story of his father's death, and the struggle of Tom and his mother to save their little home, found many listeners.

In the depot, Mr. Lenox, the ticket-agent, was telling Mr. Holmes the whole story over again — of the money Tom had saved to buy a present for his mother, of his last request as he started for the flying engine. Tears stood in both men's eyes as the recital was finished.

"Saved hundreds of lives, and thousands of dollars, by his practical knowledge. A wide-awake boy — fearless and true; risked his own life — a thorough American boy. I like him," said the general manager to the agent, in his crisp short way.

Then the special train pulled out of the depot; but Tom was not forgotten by its passengers, as the sequel will show.

Christmas day dawned bright and fair on all the world, yet there was a peculiar brightness and happiness around Tom Martin's home. Tom had purchased a rocking-chair for his mother with the money he had earned, and was contented with the past and hopeful for the future.

At ten o'clock "Doc" Wise, the express-messenger, delivered a large box at Widow Martin's home, and Tom, with all the curiosity of a wide-awake boy, soon had it open. There was a beautiful cloak from Mrs. Holmes for his mother; there was an overcoat and a suit of clothes for Tom, given by George Holmes. There was a gold watch from the general manager, bearing the inscription: "He risked his life for others. December 24, 1891." Then there was a check to pay off the mortgage, from Mr. Holmes and his guests. Last of all, in a pretty frame, was a little painting of the runaway engine, No. 303, on which Tom had taken his momentous ride. On the back of the picture was this inscription: "Be always brave and true, and you may indeed be president. MARY HOLMES." Of all the presents, Tom liked this one best.

In the evening came the men from the depot, bearing various gifts. It was a fit crowning of a happy day for Tom, because of the knowledge that he had the affection and respect of the men and boys who had known him always.

MATE BESS.
CHRISTMAS BALLAD
BY
ANNA ROBESON BROWN
ILLUSTRATED BY
FREDERICK PAPE.

Onε Christmas Eve
(so the List'ner heard),
During the reign of George the Third,
Over the road to Willoughby Hall,
Under the beeches, stiff and tall,
The Squire's coach, and his horses brown,
Bore their master from London Town:
From London Town, where a week before
The coach had stopped at a palace door,
And poor John Peter, in waistcoat fine,
Had sat and gaped at Queen Caroline.

Now, from the Court where people press,
The Squire, his wife, and their daughter Bess,
Weary, perchance, yet merry withal,
Were on their way home to Willoughby Hall.
The Squire was testy, and toss'd about,
Grumbled because his pipe was out.
My Lady's sleep was placid and sound,
And visions came, as the wheels went round
(Visions that stay'd when dreams were gone),
Of a purple silk and a gay sprigged lawn.

Bess, in her mantle of paduasoy,
Hugg'd to her bosom a fine new toy —
A slender whip with a silver head,
To startle her pony, dappled "Ned."
Now with each passing white mile-stone
The little maiden had gayer grown,
Till, in spite of the bitter freeze,
She begged "to sit by the coachman, please!"
So with joy at her novel ride,
Prattled and laughed at John Peter's side.

Sudden, from out the trees near by
Standing dark 'gainst the sunset sky,
Six black figures on horseback sped
Close on the coach. Ere a word was said,
A pistol was cocked, and a voice cried, "Stop!"
(Poor John Peter was ready to drop,
Cried out "Mercy!" and made such a fuss
They threatened him with a blunderbuss!)
The Squire, he blustered; the Lady screamed —
Something had happen'd that nobody dreamed:
Nobody thought they should have to fight
Six great robbers that very night,
Even though, just the week before,
Highwaymen halted a coach-and-four!

The Squire was gagged ere his sword was out,
All the packets were tumbled about;
The footman ran without staying to fight;
Poor John Peter was still with fright!
The Lady fainted in dire distress.
Nobody thought very much about Bess —
She had not stirred, nor screamed, nor made
Sign to show that she felt afraid;
But safe in her place, she bolder grew.
For the wise little maid saw what to do.

The robbers were careless, sure of success
(Nobody counted on little Bess).
She, who saw while the moments sped
A robber move from the horse's head,
Seized the whip, pushed the coachman back,

Hit " Brown Jerry " a sounding thwack !
Up went his nose with a snort of scorn
(This is how it was told next morn),
Flung out his hoof (so the papers said),
Hit a robber and broke his head !
Then was off with the speed of the wind,
Leaving the robbers all behind ! —
Off like mad o'er the snowy course,
Ere a robber could mount his horse !

How My Lady hugged Bess and sobbed !
How John Peter told who was robbed !
How the Squire, with pride and glee,
Cried, "She did for 'em, trouncingly !"
How old Janet, the nurse, cried "Jack !
What a marcy ye all came back !"
How maid Bess, at her father's side,
Carved the pudding at Christmas-tide —
The great big pudding with every plum
Worthy of little Jack Horner's thumb !
How her grandam and cousins five
Pledged her " the pluckiest girl alive."
The longest words could not tell it all,
The joy and the laughter at Willoughby Hall.

A LITTLE BROWN DWARF WHO SEEMED TO
BE A GUARD OVER THE TREASURES GAVE
HIM A SACK AND MOTIONED THAT MAX SHOULD
FILL IT AND EVEN HELPED HIM NEVER SAYING A
WORD

Max and the Wonder-Flower

BY JULIA D. FAY

ONG before the great king Charlemagne ruled over Germany and France, the mountain forests that border the Rhine were peopled by gnomes and dwarfs, witches and fairies, some of whom were very mischievous and could never be trusted, while others did kind deeds for the people.

They all were under the control of a fairy king, who lived in the deepest recesses of the mountains, and whose palace was so vast that it reached even under the river. On moonlight nights, the river fairies could be seen playing in the clear waters, sometimes enticing fishers to their death, by showing them gold and jewels; for the poor simple fishermen would dive down into the water and would never be seen again. But then, there were good fairies among the mountains, and these gave presents to persons whom they thought deserving of rich gifts, for the mountains were filled with treasures of gold, silver, and precious jewels; and my story is about a little boy who was rewarded by these good fairies.

He was only a poor little shepherd-boy, and tended the flocks of a rich baron, whose castle stood high up on a rock that looked down over the valley where the little boy lived. His father was dead, and he was the only help of his mother and two little sisters, Roschen and Elsie. They owned a little cottage, a goat, and a small bit of ground, which Max—for that was the boy's name—tilled in the evening, after the sheep were all safely penned for the night.

He was always cheerful, and kind to all. He loved the beautiful river that flowed along so peacefully, and the vine-terraces where grew the purple grapes. The dark forests, that seemed so still to others, filled his heart with wonder and reverence toward the great Being who had made such a lovely world.

Max longed to know how to read, so as to learn more about it all, and yet he worked on, early and late, and enjoyed even the air and the flowers; and the butterflies, as they flew by him, made him glad that he was alive.

But there came a day of sadness for poor little Max in the winter-time, for his mother was taken very ill, and the old nurse of the village, who took care of her, said that she must die unless an herb could be procured that grew in the mountains; and these were now covered with snow, beneath which the herb lay buried. But Max did not despair; he started forth, with his snow-shoes and a stout stick, to climb the mountain and find the herb that should cure his sick mother.

It was cold, and the wind blew drearily through the trees; still he tramped on boldly, until at last he stood on the summit of the mountain. The snow lay around like a soft white blanket, covering all the herbs, ferns, and flowers, keeping them warm and tucked out of sight until the spring-time. It was not very deep, and Max, with a little spade he had brought along, pushed it aside, and there was the brown earth beneath. Yet in that spot there was no herb, but before his eyes there grew a beautiful, strange flower, whiter than snow, its heart like gold, and its perfume so sweet that it seemed like a breath from the gardens of heaven. Max gazed with longing upon its beauty, and his first thought was to pluck it and take it home, that they all might see its loveliness; but his second thought was: "Oh, no; I must find first the herb for to cure mother, and then I can come here again for this flower with which to gladden her eyes." So, with a parting look, he went farther on his search, found the precious herb, and, with it safely in his pocket, came back to the spot where he had left the lovely flower.

Alas, it had disappeared! But while the tears filled his eyes, the mountain where he stood opened wide, like a door, a dazzling fairy figure appeared, and a silvery voice said:

"Enter, little Max, for thou didst first thy duty. Take what thou wilt of the treasures before thee. The Wonder-flower that thou hast seen, thou canst not take with thee. It blooms but once in a thousand years, and can only be seen by the pure in heart. Take of the gold and diamonds, love thy mother ever as now, aim to be a good man, and keep thy heart pure, that thou mayest again see the flower in the gardens of heaven, where a thousand years are but as a day."

And the fairy vanished; but around in a great marble hall shone diamonds, and rubies, and bright bars of gold, before the eyes of the bewildered Max. A little brown dwarf, who seemed to be a guard over the treasures, gave him a sack and motioned that Max should fill it, and even helped him, never saying a word. When it was filled, it was so heavy that Max wondered how he could ever carry it home; but while he hesitated, the dwarf threw it over his own shoulder, and beckoning Max to follow, crept out of the door; and as Max followed, the mountain closed behind them, and the snow lay over it as before.

It all would have seemed a dream, only that there stood the dwarf, with his pointed little hat, and strange face with eyes like a squirrel's. Not a word did he speak, but he trotted on down the mountain, and it seemed to Max scarcely an hour before they stood at its foot. There, with a bow, the dwarf set down the sack, and then he clambered up the mountain.

Max hastened home as fast as he could with his heavy treasure, and gave the nurse the herb, hiding the sack under his bed until his mother should be able to hear of his good fortune.

The herb did its work so well that in a few days his mother was able to sit up; and then Max, with his hand in hers, and his little sisters standing by him, told her all.

She clasped her hands, and said:

" My sweet child, the dear God has been very good to thee. Thou hast seen the Wonder-flower that first blossomed when Christ was born, and that no one but an innocent child may see. Keep its beauty always in mind, else the treasure it brought will give thee no happiness. Let us thank the great God of heaven for his love to thee, a poor little shepherd-boy, to whom he has shown the Wonder-flower, which even the king himself may not see!"

And it was in this strange manner that Max's wish was at last granted; for with his treasure to help him, he now could go to school and learn all about the great world outside of his little Rhine valley. He lived to be an honored and learned man, always doing good to others; and with all his wisdom he was as unassuming as a child.

A Dear Little Schemer

BY M. M. D.

HERE was a little daughter once, whose feet were — oh, so small!
That when the Christmas eve came round, they would n't do at all.
At least she said they would n't do, and so she tried another's,
And folding her wee stocking up, she slyly took her mother's.

"I 'll pin this big one here," she said — then sat before the fire,
Watching the supple, dancing flames, and shadows darting by her,
Till silently she drifted off to that queer land, you know,
Of "Nowhere in particular," where sleepy children go.

She never knew the tumult rare that came upon the roof!
She never heard the patter of a single reindeer hoof;
She never knew how Some One came and looked his shrewd surprise
At the wee foot and the stocking — so different in size!

She only knew, when morning dawned, that she was safe in bed.
"It 's Christmas! Ho!" and merrily she raised her pretty head;
Then, wild with glee, she saw what "dear old Santa Claus" had done,
And ran to tell the joyful news to each and every one:

"Mama! Papa! Please come and look! a lovely doll, and all!"
And "See how full the stocking is! Mine *would* have been too small.
I borrowed this for Santa Claus. It is n't fair, you know,
To make him wait forever for a little girl to grow."

"SHE NEVER KNEW HOW SOME ONE CAME AND LOOKED HER SELF WD SURPRISE;
AT THE WEE FOOT AND THE STOCKING — SO DIFFERENT IN SIZE."

HOW THE SECRETARY OF THE TREASURY ONCE PLAYED SANTA CLAUS.

BY SARA L GUERIN

(A True Story.)

IT was a bitter cold night in November, 1865. The Howard family, after the early supper, were gathered around the fire, laughing and chatting for an hour before the children, two little girls, Louise and Jean, went to bed.

Mr. Howard, in the big Boston rocker, was swaying gently back and forth; there was a strained, anxious look on his pleasant face, and he answered the children's many questions in an absent-minded way which was startling.

"Now, papa," said Louise, "that 's three times you have said 'Yes, dear,' when you should have said 'No.' What is the matter — are you thinking?"

"Papa is thinking very hard, deary," said the mother; "he has a hard problem to solve."

Their father looked at the two eager faces for a moment, and then said, "Come here, chicks. I will tell you all about it."

The children sprang to him, and clasping them closely in his arms, he began: "Let me see how wise and sensible you can be. You are both well-grown girls now; do you think you could make a sacrifice for our sakes — mama's and mine?"

"Oh, yes, yes! of course we could," chorused both children. "What is it?"

"Could you two little girls give up your Christmas-tree this year? Now, do you think you could?"

The curly heads drooped softly to the father's shoulder. He went on:

"It is just this way. You see, I am in the employment of the government — a servant of Uncle Sam. The war has been cruel and long; all the money has been used for the poor soldiers; so Uncle Sam has n't paid me for some months, nor, I heard at the office to-day, will he be able to do so for some time to come. Almost all my money is used up. I dare not spend a penny for anything but food and clothes for us all, dear girls; so you see a Christmas-tree and presents are out of the question. I want you both to help us bear this; for, believe me, my little lassies, 't is harder for us than it will be for you."

"Oh, papa," wailed Jean, "we 're too *little* to bear such dreadful things. Why, I 'most think I could n't live without a Christmas-tree! Why, we *always* have a *tree!*"

The father sighed as he kissed the tear-wet face of his darling. "What has my big girl to say?" he asked, looking at Louise. The brown curls were tossed back from the flushed face.

"Papa, don't mind Jeanie, she 's too little to bear things; but I 'm a big girl. Only" — here a sob was choked down —"you see we 're so *used* to it, you know."

"We will not talk about it any more to-night, for it is time to go to bed," said mama.

As the children were going slowly up the stairs, Louise heard her father say, "If the Hon. Hugh McCulloch could know how I suffer for my children's sake to-night, he would make an effort in my behalf."

Everything went wrong at school the next day. The pretty young teacher looked at Louise in amazement, for the child's thoughts seemed to be everywhere but on her lessons.

After school hours, the busy teacher looked up from her weekly reports to find Louise gazing at her intently.

"Well, dear, what is it?"

"Why, Miss Annie, I did not say anything."

"No, dear, not with words, but you know that the eyes talk. What is the trouble?"

"I want to ask some questions. I know the owner of the United States is Uncle Sam, but what 's his last name? and who is the Hon. Hugh McCulloch? and do you know where they live?"

"You funny child!" laughed Miss Graham. "I have never heard of Uncle Sam's family name, but Mr. McCulloch is an intimate friend of his — in fact, carries his purse and pays all his bills for him; and he lives in Washington."

"Oh! Well, I am going to write to him — a big letter."

"Indeed? What about, dear? Can I help you in any way?"

"You *have* helped me, Miss Annie. I think I can get it written all

right.   I — excuse me, but I can't tell you about it, because it 's something
about my father's business."

Miss Graham smiled again at the little one's dignity, but she drew the
excited child to her loving arms, and said, " That 's quite right, my dear.
Go to your desk and write your letter ; I will give you a stamp for it."

"'WHAT A BEAUTIFUL LITTLE TREE WE HAD!'"

Late that afternoon the important letter was taken to the post-office.
Don't you think the great man must have been amused when his secretary
handed him the letter, addressed in the funny, childish writing ?

I think the correspondence which was carried on by the distinguished man and the little girl will tell you best how it all ended.

Nov. 30, 1865.

DEAR MR. McKULLOCH: Won't you plese excuse me for Writing to you. I am in such trouble and want you to help me please — my papa says we can't have a chrismus tree this year, now is n't that too offley bad? He says uncle sam owes him some money and he can't get it. My papa is in the revernue busness, the revernue busness has stamps in it his name is mr henry Howard, 52 Sprague St Newark N. J. won't you plese ask him to pay him else we can't have a tree, my teacher says you pay all the bills for him. wont you ask Uncle Sam to let you pay my papa? my little sister Jeanie crys all the time, she wouldent care mutch if she was ded, she feels so bad shes so littel not to have a tree. have you got any little girls. May be the war would n't let you get paid too. I hope your little children won't have to go without any tree. Won't you plese beg uncle sam to pay up his bill to my papa plese exkuse bad speling and Writing my mamma always helps, but she dont know about this nether does my papa. Truly your littel friend,   LOUISE HOWARD.

P. S. Arent you glad the war is over.

Dec. 4, 1865.

MY DEAR LITTLE FRIEND: I was very much pleased to receive your letter. I am glad you wrote to me in your trouble, for I can and will help you.

The check for the amount the Revenue Service owes your father will be forwarded to him, without fail, by the 22d of the month — so, dear child, tell him to proceed with his arrangements for the tree. It will be all right.

I have a dear little girl like you. Her name is Louise, too. She was pleased with your letter, and wishes she could have a picture of you and little Jeanie. Can you not send her one?

Yes, my little girl will have a tree too, so I am sure of the happiness of three children, at least. Wishing you and Jeanie a Merry Christmas, I am yours sincerely,

HUGH McCULLOCH, Secretary of the Treasury.

P. S. Yes, I am very glad the war is over.

Dec. 28, 1865.

DEAR MR. McCULLOCH: My papa was so surprised when i got the big letter all sceling wax. he laughed and kissed me hard and said what a child but he was glad and so was mamma. I was so glad and so was Jeanie we both cryed, we thought mamma did too — she says she dident. oh what a beautiful little tree we had, not so big or so fine as other years, but we liked it better, ever so much better than others because we dident expect it.

You are such a kind Gentleman, do you see those round spots on this letter, they are kisses from Jean and me to you, this is our picture taken with the tree. do you like it, do you see that littel man hanging right in front,— thats george Washington, its a pen-wiper a littel boy in my fathers sunday school class made it for his chrismus gift those are my skates hanging on the tabel and thats jeanies doll, is n't she nice. Jeanie has light hair and blue eyes I have brown hair and gray eyes anser soon.

Your loving friend,   LOUISE HOWARD.

P. S. I am glad you are pleased about the war being over,— but do you know theres a dredful lot of sick soljers in our hospittel yet — I go and sing to them every saturday afternoon.

Jan. 15, 1866.

MY DEAR LITTLE LOUISE: I was more than pleased, I was delighted, with your picture. I had it on my library table on New Year's day, and it created great interest, and also admiration. The tree is beautiful, but to me your happy little faces are more so. *My* little Louise clapped her hands with joy when she saw it. I inclose to you a picture of her.

I *knew* that was George Washington before you told me. It is a striking likeness. I think that is a very nice tree for hard times.

I will close with many kind wishes for the new year — indeed, for your whole future.

Sincerely your friend,

HUGH McCULLOCH.

That was the end — no, not quite. I think if the great Secretary could have looked into the children's room at bedtime, and seen the two little white figures kneeling at their mother's knee, his heart would have glowed within him; for the ending of their prayer, said in unison, was always this:

"God bless papa and mama and Mr. Hugh McCulloch, and make Louise and Jean good girls. Amen."

Snap-shots by Santa Claus

 "I DON'T see," said Santa Claus, as he took a last look around before going out to climb into the waiting sleigh, "why I should n't take my camera with me!" So he picked it up and deposited it on the seat by his side.

Swish! — and away they went, but not so fast as usual, since "Dunder" and "Blitzen" were lame, and "Prancer" was not well.

You know what the genial old gentleman did in the present-giving way, and I mean to tell you only about a few of the pictures he took. He spoiled a good many, for they were all taken by flash-light and in a hurry. But he got one good view of a village church near which lived a favorite little boy and his two sisters; and also a picture of their stockings hanging from the holly-covered mantel.

At another house one little girl woke up when Santa Claus was taking her picture; but she thought next morning it was only a dream, so Santa Claus did n't mind having been seen.

A picture of some snowy chimneys, showing his path to and from the flue, and of the tired reindeer team, also proved successful; but a very timid

SNAP-SHOTS BY SANTA CLAUS.

little girl, and a cross black cat who snarled at Santa Claus, were frightened by the flash-light, and so spoiled their pictures.

Santa Claus took plenty of other pictures, but he does n't care to show any but these. He says it is fun to take pictures on Christmas eve.

A visit from St. Nicholas

'Twas the night before Christmas, when all through
    the house
Not a creature was stirring, not even a mouse;
The stockings were hung by the chimney with care,
In hopes that St. Nicholas soon would be there;
The children were nestled all snug in their beds,
While visions of sugar-plums danced in their heads;
And Mamma in her 'kerchief, and I in my cap,
Had just settled our brains for a long winter's nap;
When out on the lawn there arose such a clatter,
I sprang from the bed to see what was the matter.
Away to the window I flew like a flash,
Tore open the shutters and threw up the sash.
The moon on the breast of the new-fallen snow
Gave the lustre of mid-day to objects below;
When, what to my wondering eyes should appear,
But a miniature sleigh, and eight tiny rein-deer,
With a little old driver, so lively and quick,
I knew in a moment it must be St. Nick.

The original manuscript of these famous verses is in the possession of the Hon. R. S. Chilton, United States consul to Clifton, Canada, whose father was a personal friend of Mr. Moore, and who very kindly allowed us to make this facsimile copy of a page of the manuscript.

"A Visit from St. Nicholas"

any of us should happen to have an old friend whom we had never seen, we would be delighted to have his photograph, that we might know exactly how he looked.

On the opposite page is the likeness of an old friend — certainly an old friend to most of us. It is a facsimile, or exact imitation, of the original manuscript of that familiar poem which is now as much a part of Christmas as the Christmas-tree or the roast turkey and mince-pies. No matter who writes poetry for the holidays, nor how new or popular the author of such poems may be, nearly everybody reads or repeats "'T was the night before Christmas" when the holidays come round; and it is printed and published in all sorts of forms and styles, so that the new poems must stand aside when it is the season for this dear old friend. Just think of it! Jolly old St. Nicholas, with his sleigh and his reindeer and his bags full of all sorts of good things, made his first appearance to many of us in this poem. Until we had heard or read this, we did n't know much about him, except that on Christmas eve he shuffled down the chimney somehow, and filled our stockings.

Now here is a part of the poem,— as much as our page will hold,— exactly as the author, Mr. Clement C. Moore, wrote it. Here we see just how he dotted his *i*'s and crossed his *t*'s, and how he wrote some of his lines a little crookedly. If we knew nothing about Mr. Moore but what we read in the biographical notices that have been written of him, we would never suppose that he troubled his brain about St. Nicholas and his merry doings, or thought of such things as reindeer and sleighs and wild gallops over housetops. For he was a very able and learned man. He was the son of Bishop Benjamin Moore, and was born in New York, July 15, 1779. He was graduated at Columbia College (of which his father was at one time president). He was a fine Hebrew scholar, and published a Hebrew and English lexicon and a Hebrew grammar. He was afterward professor of Hebrew and Greek literature in the Protestant Episcopal Seminary in New York. He was a man of property, and had something of the St. Nicholas disposition in him, for he gave to this seminary the plot of ground on which its buildings now stand. Mr. Moore wrote many poems, which were collected and published in a book in 1844, and he did other good literary work; but he never wrote anything that will keep his memory green so long as that delightful poem on the opposite page.

Santa Claus' Pathway

BY JULIA W. MINER

NOW everywhere — not the city snow, which is so quickly trampled down and smirched, and which one gladly sees carried off in carts, certain of its swift transformation to slush and mud, but the clean, white, lasting country snow. It covered the paths, the roads, the fields, lying in great drifts against the buildings and fences; each low roof had its frozen white covering, fringed here and there with icicles; the mountains were gray to their tree-clothed summits, matching the gray sky, whence tiny flakes fell now and again.

Over the fields trudged Nan and Ned, caring nothing for snow or drifts; for on their feet were strapped big snow-shoes, and they scuffled along securely 'enough.

"First fall!" cried Ned, as Nan, inadvertently pointing her big shoe into the snow, stuck, and settled hastily and ungracefully on the ground.

"Give me your hand, Neddy. What a stupid I am!" Up she scrambled, shaking the white powder from her scarlet toboggan-suit. With the thermometer at ten degrees, there is little fear of dampness from a tumble into a drift.

"Now for a race," said Ned; "I 'll give you a start, and beat you to the little bridge."

"Thank you for nothing. You need n't give me a start, my boy, but I 'll beat you just the same. Ready!"

Off scuffled the two, Nan with a careful remembrance that her feet must be kept flat.

"Good for you, Nan!" Ned said, as his sister kept close by him. "It 'll be nip and tuck, sure enough."

Suddenly the boy's toe struck a projecting rock. Over he went, while Nan, at that moment a little in advance, pushed on unseeing. Arrived, triumphant, at the goal, she turned to look for her opponent. Half-way back sprawled a dark-gray figure; a handkerchief fluttered from one elevated foot, while close to this flag of truce stood two childish figures.

Back rushed the victor.

"Oh, Ned! Not hurt, are you?"

"Oh, no; just resting. Strap's broken. Sorry I can't rise and bow and congratulate you, ma'am. It *was* nip and tuck, was n't it? I got nipped and you tuck it." And the vanquished one sat up and proceeded to mend his snow-shoe with some string. Having offered her handkerchief and a further store of cord produced from her own pocket, Nan turned her attention to the new-comers — a boy of about her own age, and a girl several years younger.

"Good morning," she said pleasantly.

"Morning," said the girl, in a low voice.

"You're strangers in the village, are n't you?"

"Yes, we are. Father's here for his health; we've just come. Mother's going to take in washing, 'cause father can't work now."

"Find it rather cold, don't you?" said Ned.

"Yes, it's awful cold; but father likes it, and the doctor says it's good for him."

"That's so. You see, we know all about it, for we 've always lived here. We 're the doctor's children." And Nan nodded pleasantly to the two, noting their coarse yet neat clothing, and their somewhat sad young faces.

"You 're lucky to be here for the first snow," said Ned, scrambling up, and giving a stamp to test the fastenings.

"'GOOD FOR YOU, NAN!' NED SAID, AS HIS SISTER KEPT CLOSE BY HIM. 'IT 'LL BE NIP AND TUCK, SURE ENOUGH.'"

"And Christmas, you know, is the day of all the year that makes every-body feel jolly."

"We 're not going to have any Christmas this year," the girl said.

"Can't help yourselves, I guess," was Ned's cheerful reply. "December 25th brings it every time, and that 's to-morrow, sure pop!"

"Gerty means we can't have presents," joined in the boy. "But we don't mind, do we, sis? It costs a lot to get them, and it cost so much to get here, we can't hang up our stockings. We always have before, though," he added quickly.

"Dave 's real good, but I can't help minding some. I wish Christmas did n't come so expensive," Gerty sighed after a pause, during which Nan and Ned had looked at them in silence.

"Where do you live?" asked Nan, at last.

"Down that road there, 'longside o' the river, beyond the pines. First there 's a blue house, and ours is the second pink one." (Houses of many colors flourished in the little mountain village.) "Dave tried coasting down that funny open place there in the pines; it looks like a V turned upside down. He tried it on a board, and he stuck; it was too soft."

"Oh, that 's Santa Claus' Pathway," laughed Nan. Then, as the strangers stared, "That 's what we were told when we were little. You see, Santa Claus is the only person who can coast down it; I suppose the reindeer understand the road. And sometimes they run down so quickly that things drop out of the sleigh. Ned and I looked for them when we were small. Did n't we?"

"Yes, indeed; many a time. Well, good-by, youngsters. Come along, Nan."

Left alone, Gerty and Dave looked at each other a moment.

"Is n't she a beauty?" said Gerty, at last, with a long-drawn sigh. "And, oh, Davy, let 's go there and look to-morrow; will you?"

The boy laughed. "Yes, if you like," said he. "But don't expect anything; it 's only a story."

Nan's spirits were low that afternoon. The thought of the two "new" children troubled her, and she knew of nothing she could do, for her last penny had been spent in her girlish Christmas preparations, and all her available cast-off things had been contributed already to the various big packages that her kind mother made up for the poorer village folk at this time. A talk with Ned brought no balm to her spirit; like her, he was penniless. "Dead broke, my dear, and no use. Father 's advanced some of my January allowance already. But we might ask him."

"No, we must n't. Mother told me he 's given away more than he can afford now. It's hard times for him, too. I don't see why it makes any difference with a doctor, Neddy. People have to be sick just the same," she said reflectively.

Ned offered no explanation, so Nan retreated to her own pretty room to look, for the twentieth time, at the dainty, ribbon-tied packages she had prepared for the morrow. " It must be just horrid not to have any Christmas fun," she thought again.

The next day dawned bright and sunny and crisp, a perfect Christmas morning. The doctor's household was stirring betimes, for the four stockings with their abundant overflow must be inspected at an early hour, and Ned and Nan, youthful tyrants on that day, tapped early at their parents' door. Who does not know the fun of rummaging a Christmas stocking!

According to their usual custom, Dr. Lowe looked at his gifts first, being, as Ned said, "the oldest child." And few of his patients would have recognized their grave physician, as he guessed and peeped, and pulled out the presents, as eagerly as any boy. Nor was Mrs. Lowe one whit less excited when her turn followed.

" Mother and father are two spoiled children," said Ned, laughing, and casting a suspicious glance at the large package that leaned against the fireplace close to his own stocking. Could it be the wished-for toboggan? " They have so many presents, they will get to be like the little girl who had Christmas every day." For the doctor's family was remembered by nearly everybody in the village.

" What a beauty! Oh, father, how did you know I wanted it so?" cried the boy, as the new toboggan was unwrapped and admired.

Down in his stocking's deepest depths Ned found a tiny box, " From Grandma Lowe." Nan looked on with interest, for the shining five-dollar gold piece would, without doubt, have its double among her own gifts. And so it was. The girl's quick brain was busy with plans — a decision was reached at once; now the long-wanted gold beads could be bought!

Breakfast was soon over. Down the toboggan-slide and up again the children sped and clambered with untiring enjoyment. And who could grow weary of such a beauty as that new toboggan! Ned and Nan were fearless and sure of their balance, and neither could be brought to understand why their rapid rush, as they stood erect on their toboggan from top to bottom of the snow-clad hill, was considered a difficult feat by their companions.

" Get on and have a slide," said Ned, affably, noticing among the little group of onlookers the two strangers of the day before. " Hold on tight, now. If you're not used to bumps you'll fly off."

Down sped the four. Gerty's small shriek lost in the laughter her hasty rise and fall aroused. But Ned had grasped her quickly, so she was spared a tumble.

"You 'll like it better next time, so let 's try again," said he, encouragingly.

"We can't; there 's the church bell, Ned," said Nan. "We must hurry."

As Nan stooped to tie a refractory shoe-lace, she overheard Dave say to Gerty.

"Now you 've had a Christmas treat, you see, Gerty, even if we did n't find any dropped things on Santa Claus' Pathway."

Nan's toilet for church was hasty, but she and Ned were ready in time to follow their father and mother into the pretty little church, pine-trimmed and holly-decked; and Nan's clear voice rang out sweetly when the congregation sang the Christmas hymn:

> Peace on the earth, good will to men,
> From heaven's all-gracious King;
> The world in solemn stillness lay
> To hear the angels sing.

Over in the corner sat Gerty and Dave. They were singing, too, and once Nan saw Gerty stop and furtively wipe her eyes.

> "O ye, beneath life's crushing load,
> Whose forms are bending low,"

sang Nan, as she wondered. Now the meaning of the words came to her. She had not thought of it before.

The doctor's daughter did not listen to the sermon. Her Christmas sermon had been preached to her in that first hymn, and she was thinking it over seriously and not without some inward struggles. Poor Gerty and Dave! A sick father, a poor hard-working mother! Nan stole a look at her own strong, handsome, well-dressed parents, then glanced once more at the sad-looking pair in the corner. And for them there was, as Gerty had said, "no Christmas."

"But the village shops close early Christmas day, and they have so few nice things in them, anyhow," whispered a selfish little spirit in her heart. "And Grandma Lowe *meant* you to buy something for yourself with that money."

There was a little rustle as the congregation rose for the recessional:

> O holy Child of Bethlehem!
> Descend to us, we pray;
> Cast out our sin, and enter in,
> Be born in us to-day.

"NED DREW BACK, LETTING DAVE PULL OUT THE SCARLET SLED."

Nan wiped away some tears from her own eyes as she dropped on her knees.

"Ned, I want to speak to you," she whispered, almost dragging him down the church steps as the congregation filed out.

"Those Lowe children are never happy long under a roof," laughed somebody, as the two ran off on the board walk.

THE pink house down by the river was not the most cheerful place in the world that Christmas afternoon. Its few furnishings were not yet entirely unpacked; the big air-tight stove smelled of varnish; and the invalid, seated by the curtainless window, was having "one of his bad days." The poor man looked doleful enough. Sick and suffering, he felt himself the cause of his family's poverty.

"There comes the doctor's sleigh, with his pretty daughter," he said. "He rides in style. Why, it's stopping here!"

"Father sends the sleigh," began Nan, after the usual greetings, "and hopes you will like to take a little drive, as he is n't using it to-day."

The invalid glanced out at the beautiful black horses with their jingling bells and scarlet plumes, at the sleigh heaped with fur robes.

"Your father's too good, Miss," he stammered, his face flushing with pleasure.

"And perhaps Gerty and Dave might go coasting with us—Ned and me."

"Got on your boots, Dave?" queried Ned. "Then we'll go through the pines." He chatted merrily as they started off, the two girls cozily tucked up on the toboggan, the boys acting as steeds for the chariot.

Santa Claus' Pathway, like a big, white tent, stretched up by their side as they skirted the hill. "Hello!" said Ned, "er—we might climb up and see if—er—there's anything there; St. Nick might have dropped something."

"He did n't," said Gerty. "Dave and I looked." Ned and Dave exchanged glances.

"'Try, try again,'" suggested Nan. "You and I'll go, too, Gerty. It is n't deep, and it's dry as dust."

Up scrambled the youthful quartet.

"Let me talk, Ned," said Nan. "You hesitate, and they'll suspect."

"Well, how can a fellow think up things all of a sudden?" whispered Ned, in return, his tone expressing his injured feeling.

"Oh—oh! Why, look!" cried Gerty, pointing to a patch of red half hidden by the snow. "There! There! near that pine!"

The others ran forward, but Ned drew back, letting Dave pull out the scarlet sled that rewarded his search.

"Whew! That's a stunner!" cried Dave. "How did it get here? Some one must have lost it."

"Santa Claus, to be sure," cried Nan; and Ned added: "'Finding's keepings.'"

"Do you really think so?" said Dave, wistfully, unable to believe his good fortune.

"Certain sure," returned Ned. And since his own hands had put it there, who could have known better?

"Somebody told me there was n't any Santa Claus, but I guess he 's been here," said Gerty; and she nodded her head with satisfaction.

"See here!" she cried. "And they 're marked 'Gerty.'" She held up a box containing a lovely warm hood, a pair of mittens, and a box of candies as she spoke.

"Oh, goody! goody!" cried the child. "And look! here 's a game! We can play it evenings, Dave: and maybe father 'd like it, too. But," she said quickly, "you ought to take something — we must n't have them all."

"That would be unfair; we 've had our presents this morning," replied Nan. "Prob'ly these things were left here for you, for maybe Santa Claus did n't know where you 'd moved to."

This explanation seemed to satisfy Gerty, and she began to search again with fresh interest.

"These must be yours, Dave." Ned held up some mittens just as Gerty cried:

"What a love-i-ly doll! Just to think it 's mine! Oh, you dear dolly!"

"And here 's a book with my name in it," called Dave, in a few moments.

"I guess that 's all," remarked Ned, after a few minutes' further search.

"Has n't it been scrumptious?" said Gerty to Nan, as they descended the hill. And Nan thought decidedly that it had been.

"Say," said Dave to Ned, as they waited for the two girls to get settled to their liking, one on the toboggan, the other on the newly found sled, "I 'm pretty sure you and your sister put those things there. Gerty b'lieves in Santa Claus — she 's little, you see. But — I don't know how to say it — we 're awful much obliged."

Tucked up warm and snug on the toboggan, Nan was softly singing, under her breath, a joyous Christmas carol.

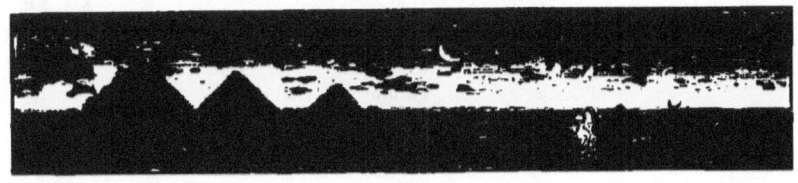

The Fool's Christmas

by Florence May Alt

On Christmas eve, the king, disconsolate,
Weary with all the round of pomp and state,
Gave whisper to his fool: "A merry way
Have I bethought to spend our holiday.
Thou shalt be king, and I the fool will be—
And thou shalt rule the court in drollery
For one short day!" With caper, nod, and grin,
Full saucily replied the harlequin:
"A merry play; and, sire, amazing strange
For one of us to suffer such a change!
But thou? Why, all the kings of earth," said he,
"Have played the fool, and played it skilfully!"
Then the king's laugh stirred all the arras dim,
Till courtiers wondered at his humor grim.

And so it chanced, when wintry sunbeams shone
From Christmas skies, lo! perched upon the throne
Sat Lionel the Fool, in purple drest,
The royal jewels blazing on his breast.

On Christmas morning, too, the king arose,
And donned, with sense of ease, the silken hose
Of blue and scarlet; then the doublet red
With azure slashed; upon his kingly head,
That wearied oft beneath a jeweled crown,
He drew the jingling hood, and tied it down.
All day he crouched amid the chill and gloom—
None seeking him—within the turret room.
But when calm night with starry lamps came down
Her purple stairs, he crept forth to the town.

His scanty cape about his shoulders blew,
Close to his face the screening hood he drew.
He knocked first at a cottage of the poor,
And lo! flew open wide the ready door.
" We have not much to give, dear fool," they said,
" But thou art cold; come share our fire and bread!"
With willing hands they freed his cape from snow,
And warmed and cheered him ere they let him go.

And so 't was ever. By the firelight dim
Of many a hearthstone poor they welcomed him;
And children who would shun the king in awe,
Would scamper to the doorway if they saw
The scarlet peak of Lionel's red hood.
" Dear fool," they called him loudly, "thou wert good
To bring the frosted cake! Come in and see
Our little Lisbeth — hark! she calls for thee!"

And so 't was ever. On his way the king
With softened heart saw many a grievous thing:
But love he found, and charity. And when
He crept at dawn through palace gates again,
He knew that he who rules by fear alone
May sit securely on his dreaded throne:
But he who rules by love shall find it true
That love, the milder power, is mightier, too.
" Dear fool," he said, "thou art a king, in sooth:
The king of hearts! To-day no farce, but truth!
For I have seen that thou, beneath my rule,
Hast often played the king.—and I the fool!"

MERRY CHRISTMAS.

M for the Music, merry and clear;
E for the Eve, the crown of the year.
R for the Romping of bright girls and boys;
R for the Reindeer that bring them the toys;
Y for the Yule-log softly aglow.

C for the Cold of the sky and the snow;
H for the Hearth where they hang up the hose;
R for the Reel which the old folks propose.
I for the Icicles seen through the pane;
S for the Sleigh-bells, with tinkling refrain.
T for the Tree with gifts all abloom;
M for the Mistletoe hung in the room;
A for the Anthems we all love to hear;
S for St Nicholas—joy of the year!

A RANDOM SHOT

BY MARION HILL.

THE "Scavenger" had gone to bed; but, as we knew from experience, far from being asleep, she was listening to every word of our conversation, and was storing it in her memory with the intention of quoting it at some future time to our discomfiture.

She was only twelve years old, and, being the youngest, was doomed to run the family errands. Though she rebelled each time she was asked to go anywhere, yet in her heart she gloried in any chance to scour the neighborhood and find out whatever was new or interesting. In her innocent babyhood she had been christened Lillian; but when, as a growing child, tucks were let out, and she began to depend upon old iron, bottles, and the contents of the rag-bag as the chief sources of her income, and consequently was forced to collect the articles of her trade with much unscrupulousness and energy, we bestowed upon her that eminently more descriptive title, the "Scavenger."

By this time you have learned that we were poor. Mother was downstairs sewing, and supposed that we four girls had gone to bed; but three of us sat before the dying fire and bemoaned our poverty.

We were Vivian, Clara, and Nan. I am Nan, the eldest of the sisters. Vivian and I have no nicknames, but Clara is called "Here," short for Hercules — a well-won honor bestowed upon her in recognition of her prowess in such feats as lifting the kitchen stove, moving the bookcase, and beating carpets.

"To be poor is hard at any time," sighed she, "but it is doubly hard at Christmas. Here it is the middle of December, and we have not a dollar."

"My heart aches for mother," said Vivian. "She is fretting herself ill over the bills."

"I should like to scalp the butcher!" murmured Here, in serious meditation.

An odd sound from the bed, a half-strangled sob, caused us to look at each other in surprise.

"What is the matter, darling?" asked Vivian, going over to the bed and trying unsuccessfully to lift from the Scavenger's face the bedclothes which were dragged over her features and clutched fiercely from beneath. "Tell your Vivian what troubles you, dear."

After being adjured several times, the grief-stricken one raised a corner of the bedclothes and sobbed forth in a roar of woe:

"Mother *is* sick! and all because she has no money. Yesterday I went into her room for some pins, and I found her on her knees by the bedside, crying and praying—*praying in the daytime!* Ow-w!" and the long-drawn sob betrayed that in the last statement she fancied her recital had reached its acme of distress.

"Don't cry, little girl; don't cry. Things may grow brighter by and by," said Vivian, soothingly, but her own voice trembled. In fact, the sudden tears also started to Clara's eyes and to mine as we guessed at the suffering our little mother had so bravely kept from us.

Vivian brushed the damp hair from the child's forehead, and petted her into a more resigned frame of mind. When she found out after a while that the much-comforted Scavenger was sobbing merely for her own private enjoyment, and reveling in the way the bed shook with each convulsive throe, Vivian came back to her old seat by the fire, and asked:

"Is there *no* way in which we girls could make a little money and help mother along? Is there *nothing* we can do?"

"We have not an accomplishment in the world," I said, a little bitterly.

"Here might give music-lessons!" said a voice from the bed, with a sobbing cackle of dismal mirth.

The sting of this suggestion lay in the fact that Clara (than whom no one had less ear for music) in moments of dejection was given to twanking viciously on an old banjo, which she played with so little melody and so much energy as to drive the rest of us to distraction.

Here broke into an amiable burst of laughter, then sank back immediately into her former state of depression.

Vivian sighed wearily, and fell into a reverie that must have been far sadder than we others could guess.

Two years before she had been engaged to be married to a young man

4

who was so affectionate, so boyish, so full of fun, that he soon won mother's
heart as completely as he had won Vivian's.   As for us girls, we simply
adored him.

"Brother Bob," for so we soon learned to call him, was summoned to
England just three months before the day set for the wedding, to take
possession of a fortune which had been left him unexpectedly.   And then
came the sad, sad news that on the vessel's return trip he was drowned.

After that news everything went wrong with us.   We gave up our Phila-
delphia home and moved to San Francisco, expecting in a vague way to
do better; but we were disappointed, and only by severest economy were we
enabled to keep a roof over us.   Poverty is a skeleton that may be kept
decently in his closet until Christmas-time; *then* he comes forth and rattles
his bones under one's very nose.

Indeed, the prospect was so dismal that it actually prevented us three tired
girls from going to bed.   We sat around the grate, looking intently at the
fire, as if trying to wrest a helpful suggestion from the fast-dropping ashes.

This second silence had lasted fully ten minutes, when it was again
cheered by a speech from the bed.

"See here," said the muffled voice.   "I have a splendid idea, but I am
afraid you — you *things* will laugh at me if you don't like it."

"Why, Lil, of course we won't!" said Vivian, reproachfully.

Thus encouraged, the flushed and blinking Scavenger struggled into a
kneeling position and addressed us with dignity :

"You know our old washerwoman, Biddy Conelly?"

Of course we did, and said so.

"You know the paper, cake, and boot-button shop she keeps?"

"Well?"

"Biddy is laid up with rheumatism, and the shop is shut."

"*Well?*"

"Well!" defiantly, as the crisis grew nearer, "why can't we keep the
shop until Biddy grows better, and make a kind of Christmas place of it
with cornucopias and Christmas-tree things, and have lots of fun, and earn
lots of money?"

Silence reigned.   Breathless and astounded, we could only look at each
other.

Then what a gabble of tongues! what a deluge of fors and againsts!
what a torrent of questions and answers! what a flavor of romance! what a
contagious excitement and freshness there was about the whole plan!

"Shopkeepers! Delightful idea! We might be able to pay all the
bills and buy mother a new dress!" said Vivian.

"I shall be able to keep my rag-money all for myself, and I 'll buy a bicycle," said the sanguine originator of the plan.

"Let us go to bed and gain the strength needed to unroll the project before mother in the morning," concluded I, with wisdom.

Well, we carried our point. Mother at first would not consent; but the gentleman who rented our front parlor spoke loudly on our side by deserting the premises without having paid his last month's bill; and we used this deplorable incident to such advantage that mother finally gave in.

Two of us rushed at once to Biddy's, and had an entirely satisfactory interview with her. Not only did she refuse to charge us rent for the shop and stock on hand, but she lent us a little money that we might lay in goods of an essentially holiday nature.

There was much to be done before we could throw open our establishment to an indulgent public. At home mother and Vivian worked untiringly — mother crocheting and knitting, Vivian dressing dolls and painting little pictures for our show-window. At the store, Lil, Clara, and I were equally busy, and afforded Biddy, who lived in rooms above, much pleasing excitement.

Clara, especially, merited much praise. Slender and girlish as she was in figure, she performed many manly feats, especially in the way of carpentry; and when it came to cleaning, the rest of us were nowhere beside her.

"Cleanliness is the thief of time," she panted; "but it 's the only way to be healthy, wealthy, and wise."

As we intended to be "shopkeepers" for two weeks only, and, moreover, as we were such comparative strangers in the city that we had no arrogant acquaintances to shock, the day on which we opened our little store found us four of the most expectant, most excited, happiest girls in the world.

Oh, you *must* hear a short description of our dear shop! It was on Third Street, almost an hour's ride from our house. It had only one show-window, and was a bakery, a confectioner's, and a stationer's, all rolled into one. But our chief pride was in our Christmas goods and tree ornaments. We considered our assortment of dolls and our stock of tin toys unrivaled; and we reached our crowning holiday effect by means of wreaths and ropes of fragrant evergreen.

At the back, opening out of the store, was a small room; and before its bright fire we sat and chatted whenever we were off duty. We made fun of everything and everybody; we roared at the poorest jokes; we were in a touch-and-go state of good humor from morning till night. Indeed, we look back upon those days as the merriest of our lives.

Our first customer! The words send a thrill through me even now. We fought so for the honor of first standing behind the counter (before the arrival of any buyer, of course) that we finally drew lots for it; and the Scavenger won. She made us retire into the back room and closed the door; then she triumphantly mounted guard alone. The bell tinkled! A child came in! We three in exile pressed our faces to the curtained glass door, and breathlessly watched the proceedings. Child pointed to a tin horse: Lil handed it

to him; child nodded; handed it back; said something; Lil wrapped horse in paper; gave it again to child; child took laboriously a coin from his stuffed pocket; laid it on counter; child went out.

Simultaneously we burst into the shop and cried: "Let us see it! Show us the money!"

"First blood for me!" shrieked the Scavenger, dashing a ten-cent piece into the till.

Vivian, who was book-keeper, entered the ten cents amid frenzied rejoicings. Soon after her first sale, Lil shoved her head into the sitting-room and observed with a quiet chuckle:

"OUR FIRST CUSTOMER."

"I say, Vivian, a young man was just straying past, and caught sight of your paintings; and they were so bad they made him ill."

"They did n't," cried Clara, indignantly.

"Did, too. He gave one look and then reeled, positively *reeled*, away."

Vivian was so used to having her pictures ridiculed that she merely smiled and said nothing.

Late in the afternoon Lillian and I were on duty together. We were very tired, all of us, for we had had an extremely busy day, the stream of customers being almost an unbroken one. Lest the uninitiated jump to the conclusion

that we were on the highroad to fortune, the explanation is necessary that
very few of the purchasers expended more than a dime at a time. Sometimes, indeed, the worth of a nickel sufficed for their modest needs. Often
we suffered the shock of seeing them go out without having bought anything
at all. To Lillian and me was vouchsafed the glory of having a customer
out of the ordinary. He came at twilight, just before the lights were lit—an
elderly-looking, heavily bearded gentleman with a gruff voice. He glanced
sharply at both of us, and then said to me in a nervous, rambling way:

" Er — ah — got any paper? note-paper? "

" Yes, sir; plenty."

" Give me — er — five dollars' worth."

" Five dollars' worth?" I repeated in amazement.

" Um — yes."

When the enormous package was at last presented to him, he paid for it
promptly, but was not yet satisfied.

" Have you — any, well, er — any nice, first-class gold pens?" he asked
again, in his uncertain fashion.

As he was looking directly at them, an answer was unnecessary, so I silently placed the tray of pens before him. He took five, at two dollars each.
I tied them up for him, blushing hotly the while, and feeling very much
ashamed; for I had come to the mortifying conclusion that he was throwing
his money into our till from benevolent motives only, and did not really
need a solitary pen or a single sheet of paper.

" Nice store — very," he said, gruffly yet affably, catching the Scavenger's glassy and dismayed stare. "Am setting up a Christmas-tree — will
want *cart-loads* of things. Have got — er — lots of children." Here he
described with his gloved hand an immense arc in the air to illustrate the
size and number of his children. "All will have to have presents. Must go
now. Will drop in again. Good-by."

The door closed behind him. Lil and I, after an astounded look at each
other, rushed into the little parlor to tell the girls.

" A nice sort of customer to have. I wish he would come again," said
Vivian.

" He 's going to; he said so."

" Was he young or old?" asked Hercules.

" Old," said I.

" Young!" said Lillian.

" He had a gray beard."

" Well, the eye part of him was young — real young," insisted Lil; and
the subject was dropped.

When the eventful, delightful day ended we ran up-stairs to bid good night to Mrs. Conelly.

"It 's a foine sthroke o' luck yez been havin'. Oi 've sot by this windy, an' it 's wan hundhred an' thirty-noine paple Oi 've counted thot 's gone in an' out o' the sture," she declared.

"Impossible!" we cried.

"Oi 've counted, and Oi know," she maintained stolidly. "Sixty-noine gone in and sixty-noine come out. Wan of thim thot wint in did n't go in at all, but kem up here and began pumpin' me about yez. Sorra a wurrud did Oi give him. Oi only tould him where yez lived, phwat yer names was, and how yez kem to be kapin' sture. Thin he tould me not to mintion him to yez, and not to tell yez whether he was a man or woman. An' Oi won't. Yez can't dhrag it out o' me."

"Did he — or she — have a long gray beard?" I asked anxiously.

"Sorra a hair on his face," she declared; adding, with a virtuous regard for truth, "barrin' an eyebrow or so."

As we could obtain no further information from her, we hurried homeward. It was charmingly dark, and we felt very independent and businesslike at being out at such an unusual hour.

Mother had a hot supper for us, and whether we ate most or talked most, she declared she could not tell.

When our hunger and excitement were both abated, we made the discovery that mother had had a little excitement of her own, and that she was trying to keep it from us. But we pounced upon her, like a pack of hyenas, with:

"Now, mother, what is it? You are a bad hand at keeping a secret. Tell us. Out with it!"

Between laughing and crying she finally told us all — that she had rented the two parlors to a very rich old gentleman, who had not only given a high price for them, but had positively paid three months in advance. She concluded by drawing a great bunch of money — real greenbacks — from her pocket and fluttering them above her head, like little flags.

Our youngest relieved her feelings in a fantastic dance.

The next day at the store was a counterpart of the first, except that the reckless buyer did not appear. For three days he kept away, but he performed prodigies when he did return. Vivian, having stayed home with mother, missed much of the fun, and had to hear second-hand a tale highly complimentary to herself; for the old gentleman bought all of her paintings, one after another, and stuffed them out of sight in his immense pockets. They seemed only to whet his appetite for more. "I will take — I want —

give me that," and he pointed abruptly and without previous consideration to the most gorgeous doll in our collection.

The poor little doll-loving Scavenger sighed deeply as she beheld her favorite go head first into one of those rapacious pockets, whence the paper-covered legs waved her a sad adieu.

Still unappeased, our customer demanded in his hearty way, "Now, then, fetch me out Christmas-tree fixings; lots, please."

At this stage of events, Hercules, who was waiting upon him, blushed a painful red, and said with meek determination: " No, sir; I 'd rather not! "

"Bless my soul!—what 's the matter with you?" demanded he, bluntly.

Through her desperation Here answered honestly: "I don't think you really want anything you are buying, sir!"

He broke into a spasm of gruff, good-natured laughter, but growled with evident sincerity that he needed all he had bought and more, and would have to go elsewhere if she refused to supply him; and on her showing him what he asked for, he purchased articles enough to decorate a banian-tree, and departed with the promise that he would "drop in to-morrow."

THE night before Christmas! We had paid all the bills; we had secretly bought mother and one another little presents; and the dear store which had enabled us to do so much was to pass into the hands of Biddy's cousin, who had come to take charge on our departure.

The delightful nervousness of Christmas eve was upon us all, and we all four were gabbling together in the center of the shop, of which we were so soon to lose possession.

"Well, I just love the old man who bought such loads of things!" exclaimed Lillian. " We would n't have done half so well but for him."

" Goodness!" said Clara, "speak of an angel and you hear his wings!"

His wings made a lot of noise, for he burst in with his usual hearty clatter; but, instead of dashing to the counter as was his wont, he stood looking steadily at Vivian, who blushed and trembled under his gaze.   And then — the dear old fellow — what did he do but rush at our lovely Vivian and clasp her in his arms!   It almost seemed that she had been put into one of those pockets, so completely did she disappear in the overcoat's embrace.

Before we, an indignant trio, had time to remonstrate, Vivian had torn herself away from him, and was looking at him less in anger than in an undefined terror, that yet was *not* terror.

" *Vivian!* My Vivian!" As his voice rang through the room, our pulses leaped with a strange remembrance, and Vivian, almost unconscious with joy, flung herself of her own free will into his arms.

Then what a crazy set we were! "Brother Bob!" "Dear Bob!" "Not drowned, but come to life again!" We shouted, we laughed, we cried; we all became like raving lunatics in our mad happiness. I found myself crying bitterly, all for no reason, over the Scavenger in a corner, while *she* was shouting, "Bob! Bob! Bob!" at intervals, like a demented calliope.

When we were the least bit calmed, Bob sent us into hysterics again by putting his wig and beard into his pocket. And then we saw the dear remembered face!

"My own, my beloved Vivian!" he cried. The glad tears were running down his face quite as freely as down ours.

Vivian said never a word, but clung to Bob's arm like one in a dream. How we got into the street we never clearly remembered, but I know we found ourselves dashing homeward at a rousing pace, and all talking together. We didn't want to be heard, we only wanted to talk. Still we were keenly conscious of Bob's narrative. He told us how he lost track of us after he was saved from the lost ship, nobody seeming to know where we had gone; how, at the end of a two years' search, a faint clue had sent him to San Francisco; how he had seen in our shop-window Vivian's painting of our old Pennsylvania home, and had recognized it; how he had learned about us from Biddy; and how he had determined to mystify us and haunt the "sture" until he could get a chance of finding Vivian behind the counter.

"Here we are at home. Don't tell us any more," commanded Lil. "Save it for mother."

On the door-step we formed, in whispers, an elaborate scheme for mother's mystification. Bob was to stay outside, while we went in and made mother believe we had brought a homeless waif with us. Then she was to go out, and bring him in to the light of her hospitable fireside; and he was to fall upon his knees and disclose himself. *Tableau!* Bob assented with cheerful readiness, and we, after a violent ring at the bell, waited in palpitating expectation.

The door opened; we crowded past mother and tried to force her away from the door, while we gabbled, "Oh, let us tell you. We knew you would n't be angry, and we brought home with us a poor old tramp with no home and no —" Here mother gently freed herself, poked her dear, pretty head out of doors, and said placidly: "Come in, Bob."

We were petrified. She knew all about it!

"Don't try to deceive your poor old mother, girls," she said, throwing open the parlor doors, and — Well, words fail me. At one end of the blazingly lighted room stood an immense Christmas-tree, dazzling with candles, and bearing on its drooping branches, besides myriads of costly gifts, every single article we had sold our "old man." It was like a child's dream of a tree. In an arm-chair by the fire sat Biddy Conelly, beaming happily upon us like a homely old fairy.

"Then Brother Bob is the 'rich old gentleman' who rented the rooms, and you knew it!" I cried, as light suddenly began to dawn upon me.

Through the blissful silence "came a still voice": "Oi did n't know thot it wor the gintleman thot died, but Oi 'm glad Oi held me tongue aboud him, or — I ax yez — where would 'a' been the surproise of it?"

But Here is looking admiringly at mother, and gasps at last: "Mama dear, I did n't know you *could* be so underhanded!"

BENEVOLENT BOY!

A very benevolent boy, Oho!
    A very benevolent boy!
He said, "O I wish I had silver and gold
    I'd fill a big house till no more it could hold
    With every nice candy and toy!"
    This exceedingly generous boy!
"And my Christmas dollar? O pshaw! don't you see?
I'll have to keep that to buy candy for me!"
    This very benevolent boy!

HO, FOR THE CHRISTMAS-TREE!

A Race with an Avalanche

BY FANNY HYDE MERRILL

OVER a little town in the heart of the Rocky Mountains floated a heavy cloud. A young girl stood by the window of one of the pretty homes, and watched anxiously the sky above. As she looked, her brother stepped up behind her. "Never mind, Kate," he said, "we 'll have a good Christmas, if it does snow."

Kate frowned. "What is the use of any more snow? It 's four feet deep on the ground now, and all the roads are blocked. We can't get any Christmas mail; the sugar in town is all gone; only one cow to give milk for the children; not an egg to be had; we can't even bake a cake!"

And just then white flakes came floating through the air. Kate's exclamation was a doleful "There it comes! It 's too bad!"

Over near the large stove sat the father. As he heard Kate's distressed voice he came to the window.

The doctor was a slender man with kind eyes and gray hair. There were many lines across his forehead, but most of them had been drawn by care and thought, few by age, and none at all by discontent. As he stood and stroked Kate's hair, it was easy to see that the young girl was the pride of his heart.

"Your mother, my dear," her father said slowly, "was always glad when it snowed at Christmas-time. She always said, 'A real Christmas should be a white Christmas.'"

Tears stood in Kate's eyes, and Harry turned away his head. He did not wish Kate to know how desolate home had been to him since their mother's death.

Through the gathering snow two heavy figures came toward the house. Harry opened the door, and saw two strong men with resolute faces.

"Does Dr. Ward live here?" they asked.

The doctor stepped forward. In spite of the storm, the men lifted their caps as they saw his face.

"There 's a man hurt up at the mines," said the taller of the two men. "Will you come up, doctor?"

"Certainly," said the doctor, promptly. "I 'll come at once."

The man looked at the two young people. "Doctor," he said, "you know the snow is sliding badly? It 's a deal of risk."

The doctor nodded, and put on his thick coat.

"Oh, papa!" cried Kate, "not to-day! Not you! We can't let you go." In distress she turned to the men: "Can't you get some younger man for such a hard trip?"

The man looked troubled. "I 'm sorry, Miss; we did try. "But"— his face hardening—"no other doctor will go. And the man is badly hurt."

Poor Kate! Father and brother had hidden their own grief over the mother's death, and striven to make her life bright. Now she could not believe she could be put aside for any other call. She clung to her father, sobbing.

"Kate," he said, as he took her hands, "my work is to *save* lives —"

"But, papa! your life — so useful — save *that!*"

"My dear, who can tell which life is most needed? Besides, your fears are foolish, dear. There is probably no real danger. I shall come back safely, never fear." He stopped with his hand on her head. Then, satchel in hand, he went to the door. As he stepped across the threshold he took Harry's hand. "My boy," he said, "you are like your mother. I can trust Kate to you"; and the door closed. The three men plowed their way up the street into the mountain trail that led to the mines. Kate watched the figures grow small in the distance, till the snow hid them from sight. The mighty hills that shut in the town never looked to Kate so high, so silent, so unmoved as during the long hours of that day. In vain Harry planned diversions: she watched the window with an anxious and a sorrowful face. Still the storm raged; and, as the twilight gathered, Harry could not keep anxiety from his face and voice.

Down in the valley the twilight fades early, and it was dark when a heavy rap brought Harry to the door. There stood twelve men, and in their midst, on a sled, an uncouth mass of snow-covered blankets.

"Where's father?" gasped Harry, staring at the sled with its heavy burden.

"He said we were to tell you the storm was so bad he'd stay up at the mine to-night. We're taking the fellow that was hurt down to the hospital."

"Noble fellows!" cried Harry, with his face aglow, as the men set off again. "Those twelve men have brought that hurt fellow down the mountain on a sled in this storm and darkness, over four feet of snow. They faced death every step of the way, for the snow is sliding all the time."

Kate stared at the fire, but said nothing. Suddenly a veil had been lifted. She saw not only her noble father risking his life for others,— that was no new vision,— but the rough, the faithful miners, twelve of them, risking their lives to carry to greater safety one poor, hurt, perhaps dying, man. And she —all day long she had brooded over her own selfish sorrow and anxiety, letting Harry try to amuse her, but never thinking of his troubles.

With a flush of shame she started up.

"Harry," she said, "we'll practise a little to-night; can't we?"

And Harry brought out his flute and the music with a face of such relief and happiness that Kate's heart gave another throb of remorse.

The morning of the next day dawned clear and cool. Gradually the sun rose over the mountains, each moment touching into new glory the light and shadow, the color and glittering sheen, of the vast snow-covered hills. Kate sang over her morning work, and thought tenderly of the new comfort she would bring into her father's life from that day forward. Nine o'clock it was before the sunlight touched the town in the valley. Harry began to watch the mountain trail for his father. All day long the "beauty of the hills" glittered before the longing eyes of Kate and Harry, but no father came down the shining mountain path. At three o'clock the sun went down, and the tints of sunset glowed upon the snowy heights. Kate bravely struggled through the pretense of a meal; but self-control is not learned in a day, and by evening Harry found her crying softly by herself.

"Kate," he said, "don't worry; to-morrow I 'll go up the mountain and see if father is still there."

Harry started early, next morning, and Kate bravely watched him out of sight.

"We 'll be home for Christmas," he shouted back, for his spirits rose with the prospect of something to do. He climbed to the mines, and found, to his dismay, that his father had started down early the preceding morning, the superintendent having watched him out of sight.

"Well," said Harry, "I must go down and get up a party from town to search for him."

"That is the best way," said the manager.

He said nothing of the danger Harry himself must pass through. Danger was around them all.

Harry was strong, active, and skilful in the use of the snow-shoes, or skees, which he wore that day.

The boy's face was saddened by his fears for his father, but a resolute look flashed into his eyes as he made ready for the perilous trip. Just as he shot forward, came the thunder of a blast of dynamite in the mine above him. A shout went up, "A snow-slide!" and a mass of snow, dislodged by the explosion, came crushing past. A corner of the shed containing the men was carried away. The men looked at each other. Their escape had been narrow; where was the boy who had just now shot forward in the very path of the avalanche?

It needed no shout to tell Harry what the result of that report would be. He had started, and almost at that instant the snow was on his track. There was no chance for turn or thought of pause. His only chance for life was to reach the valley before the avalanche.

Over the shortest, steepest descent he flew, the wind cutting his face, all thought merged in one fire of effort to fly faster.

Faster, faster, he skimmed the glittering snow, till he shot like an arrow from a bow into the plain below, and fell headlong covered by the frosty spray at the edge of the spent avalanche. The breath seemed pressed out of his body, and for some minutes he did not move.

Then a shout came through the air, and he lifted himself as a band of miners came flying down the mountain toward him. They came on snow-shoes from the mines above, and were overjoyed to find the boy alive. "He beat the snow-slide!" they ejaculated, and Harry, a hero from that hour, was escorted home in triumph.

At the door stood Kate, and back of her the good father, safe and sound. On his way down from the mine, the doctor had been hailed by a man who lived in a little cabin sheltered in the mountain-side. The man's child had broken an arm, and by the time everything was done for his relief, the short day was so far gone that the doctor was obliged to stay all night.

That Christmas eve, as Kate and Harry and their father stood watching the stars glow and sparkle in the keen mountain air, Kate put her hand on her father's arm as she said: "There won't be much for Christmas to-morrow; but any other happiness that could come to me would seem very small, after having you and Harry given back to me."

"My dear," said her father, "since the

HARRY'S RACE FOR LIFE.

Christmas angels first sang 'Peace on earth, good will toward men,' the best gift that can come to any of us is an unselfish heart."

"CHIME, CHIME, CHIME,—S'CH A MERRY LOAD
SLEIGHING IN THE MOONLIGHT ALONG THE RIVER ROAD!"

The Christmas Sleigh-Ride

BY HELEN GRAY CONE

THEY started from the old farm-gate,
    The happiest boys alive,
With Rob, the roan, and Rust, his mate,
    And Uncle Jack to drive;
The snow was packed, that Christmas-time,
    The moon was round and clear,
And when the bells began to chime,
    They all began to cheer.
Chime, chime, chime, chime,—such a merry load
Sleighing in the moonlight along the river road!

They passed the lonely cider-mill,
    That 's falling all apart;
The hermit heard them on the hill,—
    It warmed his frozen heart;
They cheered at every farm-house gray,
    With window-panes aglow,—
Within, the farmer's wife would say,
    "Well, well, I want to know!"
Chime, chime, chime, chime,—such a noisy load
Speeding by the homesteads along the river road!

The river shone, an icy sheet,
    As o'er the bridge they flew;
Then down the quiet village street
    Their Christmas horns they blew;
The sober people smiled and said,
    "We 'll have to give them leave
(Boys will be boys!) to make a noise,
    Because it 's Christmas eve!"
Chime, chime, chime, chime,—such a lively load
Scattering songs and laughter along the river road!

But now it 's growing hard to keep
    Awake, and now it seems
The very bells have gone to sleep,
    And jingle in their dreams.
The lane at last,—the farm-gate creaks,
    And Grandma cries, "It 's Jack!
Why, what a peck of apple-cheeks
    These boys have brought us back!"
Chime, chime, chime, chime,—such a hungry load,
Rosy from the Christmas ride along the river road!

A·New·Fashioned· Christmas

BY JULIE M. LIPPMANN

We had been busy talking, for hours, Christmas eve,
Of all the great improvements until — will you believe ? —
I felt quite dull and drowsy, and said, 'twixt yawn and sigh,
"Oh! anything old-fashioned had best pass out and die!"

And then I leaned back smiling and quite self-satisfied,
And closed my eyelids slowly, when, lo! they opened wide
In sheer amaze and wonder, and would you know the cause?
I saw before me standing, the form of Santa Claus.

But, oh! so strange and altered! In clothes of latest style,
And not at all the Santa I 'd dreamed of all the while.
But still I recognized him, and said: "I did n't see
You come out from the chimney, — 't was very dull of me."

"The chimney ?" said he gruffly, "I beg of you to know
I clamber down no chimneys; I stopped that long ago!"
I said, "Your load was heavy, you 're tired; won't you rest ?"
"Oh, no," he answered grandly, "my goods were all expressed!"

" You must have found it pleasant — the sleighing, sir, I mean.
  The roofs are much more snowy than I have ever seen."
" Indeed ! " — his air was lofty — " 't is not the present mode
  To drive a sleigh.   I travel by the elevated road."

'T was all so strange it chilled me, but still I said, " Now, please,
You won't forget to send us one of your Christmas-trees.
The children love you dearly and try to be *so* good."
He said : " No trees hereafter, I 'd have it understood.

" In fact, the time is over for Christmas. I should say
  Those very old-time customs have really passed
          away.
  We want the very latest, dear madam, you
          and I,
  And peace, good will, and Christmas are
          of a time gone by."

And then he seemed preparing to take
      his leave and go.
But do you think I let him? I called
      out bravely, " No ! "
I ran to him and begged him, between
      my sobs and tears,
To leave us blessed Christmas, just as in
      former years.

To change no little custom ; to take no
      part away ;
To leave us dear old-fashioned, beloved
      Christmas day.
And then, for just an instant, my
      eyes were very dim
With tears, and when I cleared
      them, I saw a change in
      him :

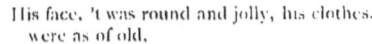
"Oh, no," he answered grandly," my goods were all expressed,

His face, 't was round and jolly, his clothes,
        were as of old,
He had a pack upon his back as full as it could
        hold.
And as he beamed upon me I heard his reindeer prance,
Then sly old Santa gave me a smile and roguish glance.

"I wish you Merry Christmas ! " I thought I heard him say.
And when I tried to answer him, he 'd vanished quite away !
But though they say I dreamed it, I know we shall have still
Our dear old-fashioned Christmas, bringing " Peace on earth, good will ! "

Where the Christmas-tree grew

BY MARY E. WILKINS

IT was afternoon recess at No. 4 District School, in Warner. There was a heavy snow-storm, so every one was in the warm school-room, except a few adventurous spirits who were tumbling about in the snow-drifts out in the yard, getting their clothes wet and preparing themselves for chidings at home. Their shrill cries and shouts of laughter floated into the school-room, but the small group near the stove did not heed them at all. There were five or six little girls, and one boy. The girls, with the exception of Jenny Brown, were trim and sweet in their winter dresses and neat school-aprons. They perched on the desks and the arms of the settee with careless grace, like birds. Some of them had their arms linked. The one boy lounged against the blackboard. His dark, straight-profiled face was all aglow as he talked. His big brown eyes gazed now soberly and impressively at Jenny, then gave a gay dance in the direction of the other girls.

"Yes, it does — *honest !* " said he.

The other girls nudged one another softly; but Jenny Brown stood with her innocent, solemn eyes fixed upon Earl Munroe's face, drinking in every word.

"You ask anybody who knows," continued Earl; "ask Judge Barker; ask — the minister —"

"Oh !" cried the little girls; but the boy shook his head impatiently at them.

"Yes," said he; "you just go and ask Mr. Fisher to-morrow, and you 'll see what he 'll tell you. Why, look here,"— Earl straightened himself and stretched out an arm like an orator,— "it 's nothing more than *reasonable* that Christmas-trees grow wild with the presents all on 'em ! What sense would there be in 'em if they did n't, I 'd like to know ? They grow in different places, of course; but these around here grow mostly on the mountain over there. They come up every spring, and they all blossom out about Christmas-time, and folks go hunting for them to give to the children. Father and Ben are over on the mountain to-day —"

"Oh, oh!" cried the little girls.

"I mean I guess they are," amended Earl, trying to put his feet on the boundary-line of truth. "I hope they 'll find a full one."

Jenny Brown had a little, round, simple face; her thin brown hair was combed back and braided tightly in one tiny braid tied with a bit of shoe-string. She wore a nondescript gown, which nearly trailed behind, and showed in front her little coarsely shod feet, which toed in helplessly. The gown was of a faded green color; it was scalloped and bound around the bottom, and had some green-ribbon bows down the front. It was, in fact, the discarded polonaise of a benevolent woman, who aided the poor substantially but not tastefully.

Jenny Brown was eight, and small for her age — a strange, gentle, ignorant little creature, never doubting the truth of what she was told, which sorely tempted the other children to impose upon her. Standing there in the school-room that stormy recess, in the midst of that group of wiser, richer, mostly older girls, and that one handsome, mischievous boy, she believed every word she heard.

This was her first term at school, and she had never before seen much of other children. She had lived her eight years all alone at home with her mother, and she had never been told about Christmas. Her mother had other things to think about. She was a dull, spiritless, reticent woman, who had lived through much trouble. She worked, doing washings and cleanings, like a poor feeble machine that still moves but has no interest in its motion. Sometimes the Browns had almost enough to eat; at other times they half starved. It was half-starving time just then; Jenny had not had enough to eat that day. There was a pinched look on the little face upturned toward Earl Munroe's.

Earl's words gained authority by coming from himself. Jenny had always regarded him with awe and admiration. It was much that he should speak at all to her.

Earl Munroe was quite the king of this little district school. He was the son of the wealthiest man in town. No other boy was so well dressed, so gently bred, so luxuriously lodged and fed. Earl himself realized his importance, and had at times the loftiness of a young prince in his manner. Occasionally some independent urchin would bristle with democratic spirit, and tell him to his face that he was "stuck up," and he had n't so much more to be proud of than other folks — that his grandfather was n't anything but an old ragman !

Then Earl would wilt. Arrogance in a free country is likely to have an unstable foundation. Earl's tottered at the mention of his paternal grandfather, who had given the first impetus to the family fortune by driving a tin-cart about the country. Moreover, the boy was really pleasant and generous-hearted, and had no mind, in the long run, for lonely state and disagreeable haughtiness. He enjoyed being lordly once in a while, that was all.

He did now, with Jenny. He eyed her with a gay condescension which would have greatly amused his tin-peddler grandfather.

Soon the bell rang, and they all filed to their seats, and the lessons were begun.

After school was done that night, Earl stood in the door when Jenny passed out.

"Say, Jenny," he called, "when are you going over on the mountain to find the Christmas-tree? You 'd better go pretty soon, or they 'll be gone."

"That 's so," chimed in one of the girls. "You 'd better go right off, Jenny."

She passed along, her face shyly dimpling with her little innocent smile, and said nothing. She would never talk much.

She had quite a long walk to her home. Presently, as she was pushing weakly through the new snow, Earl went flying past her in his father's sleigh, with the black horses and the fur-capped coachman. He never thought of asking her to ride. If he had, he would not have hesitated a second before doing so.

Jenny, as she waded along, could see the mountain always before her. This road led straight to it, then turned and wound around its base. It had stopped snowing, and the sun was setting clear. The great white mountain was all rosy. It stood opposite the red western sky. Jenny kept her eyes fixed upon the mountain. Down in the valley shadows, her little simple face, pale and colorless, gathered another kind of radiance.

There was no school the next day, which was the one before Christmas. It was pleasant, and not very cold. Everybody was out; the little village stores were crowded; sleds trailing Christmas greens went flying; people with parcels under their arms, their hands full.

Jenny Brown also was out. She was climbing Franklin Mountain. The snowy pine boughs bent so low that they brushed her head. She stepped deeply into the untrodden snow; the train of her green polonaise dipped into it and swept it along. And all the time she was peering through those white fairy columns and arches for — a Christmas-tree.

That night the mountain had turned rosy, and faded, and the stars were coming out, when a frantic woman, panting, crying out now and then in her distress, went running down the road to the Munroe house. It was the only one between her own and the mountain. The woman rained some clattering knocks on the door — she could not stop for the bell. Then she burst into the house, and threw open the dining-room door, crying out in gasps:

"Hev you seen her? Oh, hev you? My Jenny's lost! She's lost! Oh, oh, oh! They said they saw her comin' up this way, this mornin'. *Hev* you seen her? *Hev* you?"

Earl and his father and mother were having tea there in the handsome oak-paneled dining-room. Mr. Munroe rose at once, and went forward; Mrs. Munroe looked with a pale face around her silver tea-urn; and Earl sat as if frozen. He heard his father's soothing questions, and the mother's answers. She had been out at work all day; when she returned, Jenny was gone. Some one had seen her going up the road to the Munroes' that morning about ten o'clock. That was her only clue.

Earl sat there, and saw his mother draw the poor woman into the room and try to comfort her; he heard, with a vague understanding, his father order the horses to be harnessed immediately; he watched him putting on his coat and hat out in the hall.

When he heard the horses trot up the drive, he sprang to his feet. When Mr. Munroe opened the door, Earl, with his coat and cap on, was at his heels.

"Why, you can't go, Earl!" said his father, when he saw him. "Go back at once."

Earl was white and trembling. He half sobbed. "Oh, father, I must go!" said he.

"Earl, be reasonable. You want to help, don't you, and not hinder?" his mother called out of the dining-room.

Earl caught hold of his father's coat. "Father — look here. I — *I believe I know where she is!*"

Then his father faced sharply around, his mother and Jenny's stood listening in bewilderment, and Earl told his ridiculous, childish, and cruel little story. "I — did n't dream — she 'd really be — such a little — goose as to — go," he choked out; "but she must have, for" — with brave candor — "I know she believed every word I told her."

It seemed a fantastic theory, yet a likely one. It would give method to

the search, yet more alarm to the searchers.   The mountain was a wide
region in which to find one little child.

Jenny's mother screamed out, "Oh, if she 's lost on the mountain,
they 'll never find her! They never will, they never will! O Jenny, Jenny,
Jenny!"

Earl gave a despairing glance at her, and bolted up-stairs to his own
room. His mother called pityingly after him; but he only sobbed back,
"Don't, mother — please!" and kept on.

"THIS LITTLE GIRL CAME FLYING OUT WITH HER CONTRIBUTION; THEN THERE WERE MORE."

The boy, lying face downward on his bed, crying as if his heart would
break, heard presently the church bell clang out fast and furious.   Then he
heard loud voices down in the road, and the flurry of sleigh-bells.   His
father had raised the alarm, and the search was organized.

After a while Earl arose and crept over to the window.   It looked toward the mountain, which towered up, cold and white and relentless, like
one of the ice-hearted giants of the old Indian tales.   Earl shuddered as he
looked at it.   Presently he crawled down-stairs and into the parlor.   In
the bay-window stood, like a gay mockery, the Christmas-tree.   It was a
quite small one that year, only for the family, — some expected guests had
failed to come, — but it was well laden.   After tea the presents were to

have been distributed. There were some for his father and mother, and some for the servants, but the bulk of them were for Earl.

By and by, his mother, who had heard him come down-stairs, peeped into the room, and saw him busily taking his presents from the tree. Her heart sank with sad displeasure and amazement. She would not have believed that her boy could be so utterly selfish as to think of Christmas presents *then*.

But she said nothing. She stole away, and returned to poor Mrs. Brown, whom she was keeping with her. Still she continued to think of it all that long, terrible night, when they sat there waiting, listening to the signal-horns over on the mountain.

Morning came at last, and Mr. Munroe with it. No success so far. He drank some coffee and was off again. That was quite early. An hour or two later the breakfast-bell rang. Earl did not respond to it, so his mother went to the foot of the stairs and called him. There was a stern ring in her soft voice. All the time she had in mind his heartlessness and greediness over the presents. When Earl did not answer, she went up-stairs, and found that he was not in his room. Then she looked in the parlor, and stood staring in bewilderment. Earl was not there, but neither was the Christmas-tree nor his presents. They had vanished bodily!

Just at that moment Earl Munroe was hurrying down the road, and he was dragging his big sled, on which were loaded his Christmas presents and the Christmas-tree. The top of the tree trailed in the snow; its branches spread over the sled on either side, and rustled. It was a heavy load, but Earl tugged manfully in an enthusiasm of remorse and atonement, —a fantastic, extravagant atonement, planned by that same fertile fancy which had invented that story for poor little Jenny, but instigated by all the good, repentant impulses in the boy's nature.

On every one of those neat parcels, above his own name, was written in his big, crooked, childish hand, "Jenny Brown, from —." Earl Munroe had not saved one Christmas present for himself.

Pulling along, his cheeks brilliant, his eyes glowing, he met Maud Barker. She was Judge Barker's daughter, and the girl who had joined him in advising Jenny to hunt on the mountain for the Christmas-tree.

Maud stepped along, placing her trim little feet with dainty precision. She wore some new, high-buttoned overshoes. She also carried a new beaver muff, but in one hand only. The other dangled mittenless at her side; it was pink with cold, but on its third finger sparkled a new gold ring with a blue stone in it.

"Oh, Earl!" she called out, "have they found Jenny Brown? I was going up to your house to— Why, Earl Munroe, what have you got there?"

"I 'm carrying my Christmas presents and the tree up to Jenny's—so she 'll find 'em when she comes back," said the boy, flushing red. There was a little defiant choke in his voice.

"Why, what for?"

"I rather think they belong to her more 'n they do to me, after what 's happened."

"Does your mother know?"

"No. She would n't care. She 'd think I was only doing what I ought."

"All of 'em?" queried Maud, feebly.

"You don't s'pose I 'd keep any back?"

Maud stood staring. It was beyond her little philosophy.

Earl was passing on, when a thought struck him.

"Say, Maud," he cried eagerly, "have n't you something you can put in? Girls' things might please her better, you know. Some of mine are — rather queer, I 'm afraid."

"What have you got?" demanded Maud.

"Well, some of the things are well enough. There 's a lot of candy and oranges and figs and books; there 's one by Jules Verne I guess she 'll like. But there 's a great big jack-knife, and — a brown-velvet bicycle suit."

"Why, Earl Munroe! what could she do with a bicycle suit?"

"I thought, maybe, she could rip the seams to 'em, an' sew 'em some way, an' get a basque cut, or something. Don't you s'pose she could?" Earl asked anxiously.

"I don't know; her mother could tell," said Maud.

"Well, I 'll hang it on, anyhow. Maud, have n't you anything to give to her?"

"I — don't know."

Earl eyed her sharply. "Is n't that muff new?"

"Yes."

"And that ring?"

Maud nodded. "She 'd be delighted with 'em. Oh, Maud, put 'em in!"

Maud looked at him. Her pretty mouth quivered a little; some tears twinkled in her blue eyes.

"I don't believe my mother would let me," faltered she. "You — come with me, and I 'll ask her."

"All right," said Earl, with a tug at his sled-rope.

He waited with his load in front of Maud's house until she came forth radiant, lugging a big basket. She had her last winter's red cashmere

dress, a hood, some mittens, some cake and biscuit, and a few nice slices
of cold meat. "Mother said these would be much more *suitable* for her,"
said Maud, with a funny little imitation of her mother's manner.

Over across the street, another girl stood at the gate, waiting for news.

"Have they found her?" she cried. "Where are
you going with all those things?"

Somehow, Earl's gen- erous, romantic impulse
spread like an epidemic. This little girl soon
came flying out with her con- tribution; then there
were more — quite a little procession filed finally
down the road to Jenny Brown's house.

The terrible possibilities of the case never occurred to them. The idea never entered their
heads that little, innocent, trustful Jenny might
never come home to see that Christmas-tree
which they set up in her poor home.

It was with no surprise
whatever that they saw,
about noon, Mr. Munroe's
sleigh, containing Jenny
and her mother and
Mrs. Munroe, drive up
to the door.

Afterward they
heard how a wood-
cutter had found Jenny
crying, over on the
east side of the moun-
tain, at sunset, and had
taken her home with
him. He lived five
miles from the village,
and was an old man,
not able to walk so
far that night to tell
them of her safety.

"ALL TOO FAR AWAY HAD SHE BEEN SEARCHING FOR THE CHRISTMAS-TREE."

His wife had been very good to the child. About eleven o'clock some of
the searchers had met the old man plodding along the mountain road with
the news.

They did not stop for this now. They shouted to Jenny to "come in,

quick!" They pulled her with soft violence into the room where they had
been at work. Then the child stood with her hands clasped, staring at
the Christmas-tree. All too far away had she been searching for it. The
Christmas-tree grew not on the wild mountain-side, in the lonely woods,
but at home, close to warm, loving hearts; and that was where she found it.

SANTA CLAUS PUZZLED AT LAST.
" These apartment-houses are too much for me!"

How a Street-Car Came in a Stocking

BY HARRIET ALLEN

"'I'LL TELL YOU WHAT IT IS. IT'S ALL
ABOUT A STREET-CAR.'"

DAVID DOUGLAS wanted to be a street-car driver. That did not interfere in the least with his ambition to be a plumber with a bag of tools, or a doctor with a pocket-thermometer and a stop-watch. David was almost seven years old. He had been in love with the street-car profession for at least a year; and there was nothing he could n't tell you about that business which *can* be told to an outsider whose heart is not in it.

Yet there was nothing remarkable about David. He could read and write as well as other boys of his age, and he spelled with less originality perhaps than most. He could run as fast, jump as far, and spin tops with the best. Although David had neither brother nor sister to play with, and no nursery full of toys, he managed to have a lot of fun, and he had a rather manly sort of character. As to playfellows—nobody could excel his mother. She rode in his express-train, and had her ticket punched till there was nothing left of it; and when the engineer struck a broken rail, she was a passenger in the wreck, and he bandaged her up with handkerchiefs and old string until you would n't have known her. Then, too, she had that rare faculty of knowing, from a boy's point of view, a funny thing when she saw it, and sometimes they laughed together till the tears rolled down their cheeks.

Then there was "Jack." I nearly forgot him. He was David's beloved dog. Jack was a short-haired yellow dog without pedigree or family connections — what might be called a self-made dog. He owed his present home and success in the world to self-respecting enterprise and a kind heart. Jack was ever cheerful and cheery, fond of exercise and excitement, and always on hand.

Now, David's father had a habit of reading aloud to David's mother, before breakfast, from the morning paper.

One morning, about three weeks before Christmas, David was transfixed by hearing his father read the following announcement:

CARS TO GIVE AWAY

An Offer of the Street-Car Company

General Manager Miller, of the Citizens' Street-Railroad Company, said to-day that he had on hand thirty or forty old box street-cars which he would like to give away. The company has no further use for the cars. Mr. Miller suggests that the cars would make good play-houses for children.

Do you wonder that such a notice sent David's appetite flying?

"Oh, papa," he cried, "let us get one of those cars!" whereupon his father made big eyes of astonishment at David, and pretended to be absolutely upset by the mere suggestion of such an idea, and was in such wild haste to get out of reach of little boys who wanted to have full-grown, real street-cars for their very own, that David was unable to get in a serious word before he was gone. But David's eyes were shining and his fancy was building the most beautiful castles. He took his cap and disappeared with Jack.

Some hours later he came in glowing from the cold air, and saying enthusiastically, "Mama, I know where we can put that car, if we *should* get it — in our side yard! You can just come to the window and see! There's plenty of room — I 've marked it out on the snow."

"My dear little boy! Did you really think we could ask for one of those cars?"

David's face flushed; he certainly had hoped so; he had spent the morning thinking about it. "I did n't know," he faltered, with a sense of bereavement tugging at his heart.

"That 's too bad! I do wish you could have one to play in, David!"

"Why can't I, mama?"

"It would cost too much, dear."

"Cost too much? Why, mama," he said, brightening up, "did n't you hear? The paper said they would give them away."

"So they will — but even a present is sometimes expensive. You see, it would cost a great deal to bring a street-car all the way over here and set it up in our yard."

"Why, mama?" and his lip trembled. He did so want that car, and it had looked so easy!

"Because a street-car is so large and so heavy, it would take strong horses, and a great big truck, and ever so many men to move it; and all that costs money — a great deal of money."

Very gently she convinced him that it was out of the question. If you could n't afford a thing — there you were! Yet it seemed a thousand pities — thirty or forty cars to be *given* away! It was very comforting at this point to have his mother thump him confidingly on the back, as she said that he was the bravest little man in all the world; and to be asked what he expected Santa Claus to bring him, and whether he meant to hang up Jack's stocking, too.

David had a good many Christmas wishes: a bob-sled, for one thing, and skates, and a gun to shoot a dart; and he longed for a hook-and-ladder wagon, or, failing that, a police-patrol with a real gong on the front. It was quite impossible to choose, so he had sent the entire list to Santa Claus in a letter just to see what would happen.

But that night, as his mother tucked him into bed, he held her back by the hand and said hesitatingly: "Mama, why could n't they bring the car around here on the track that runs in front of our house?"

"Because those cars have no wheels."

"No wheels!"

"Not a wheel, sir! It would just be a helpless old car all the rest of its life"; and she shook her hand free, gave him a little pat, a good-night kiss, and was gone.

Not far from David there lived a little boy whose name was Harold Wolfing; he was not quite five years old. He was a sturdy little fellow, with dark hair and eyes, and a fine red in his cheeks; and he carried his head and shoulders in quite a military fashion. He was fortunate enough to live in the same house with his grandmama and grandpapa. Whether they were equally fortunate in this arrangement is a matter I never heard discussed; but certainly they loved and petted him, and he had four aunties and three uncles — all of whom seemed really to lie awake nights thinking what they could give him next.

Harold was very fond of having David come to play, and, it is needless

to say, David was very fond of going.   David liked nothing better than to
ride the high-headed hobby-horse, and to work the fire-engine that squirted
real water through a rubber hose.

One day, not long before Christmas, David went to spend the afternoon
with Harold.   He found the chubby little man bending over his nursery
table, busy with pencil and paper.

"Do you know what I 'm doin', David?   I 'm writin' a letter!"   A
moment was allowed for this fact to
impress the smiling David, then —
"Who do you think I 'm writin' to?"

David said promptly that he
could n't guess.

"Santa Claus!   You can read
it if you want to," added the
writer, condescendingly.   David
took the letter, which was
covered with mysterious,
wandering pencil-
marks.   He was
quite embarrassed
to know what to
say to such a baby,
who could not even
print; but Harold
relieved   him.
"Can't you read,
David?" he said
pityingly.   "Here,
I 'll read it to you."
And he took the
letter back into his
fat little hand with
an important air.
After studying it
very hard for a

"'DAVID, IF CHILDREN ASK TOO MUCH, SANTA CLAUS MUST
DISAPPOINT THEM.'"

moment, he fixed David with his eye, saying: "It 's *very* long, David,
it 's very long; but never mind, I 'll tell you what it says.   It 's all about
a street-car.   You see, I 'm goin' to have Santa Claus bring me a street-car
for Christmas."   He spoke of the arrangement with such assurance that
David suddenly felt himself very young and inexperienced.

" Yes," he went on, highly pleased with the impression he was making —
" yes; I 'm goin' to have a street-car. Perhaps you think it 's goin' to be
little, like that? "— pointing to a toy car.

David did n't know.

" Well, it is n't. It is a *real* car, and as large — oh, almost a large as
this house! You can come and play in it, David; and I 'll take you to ride,
all the way out to the park, and clear out — clear out to the end of the
world — and I 'll drive as *fast* — oh, so you can hardly hold on! Only,"—
and he pulled in his fancy a little, lest David's go too far,—" you 'll be *inside*, you know, and I 'll ring the bell when you pay me." Exciting as this
picture was, David's mind flew back at once to the forty cars to be given
away. Was Harold's car one of these? Hardly, he thought; since Harold
looked to Santa Claus for his, and those cars belonged to the Street-Railroad Company. He decided to settle the doubt. " Where will Santa Claus
get a street-car? " he asked. Harold gave him a look of astonished reproach.

" Why, don't you know Santa Claus can get anything he wants, and he 'll
bring it to you if you ask him, and if you 're good? "

David did know something very like this, and now on a sudden an idea
flashed into his mind that made his heart jump and sent the color flushing
up to his short yellow curls; it was this: You see, if Santa Claus was giving street-cars away, there was nothing to pay for hauling. No need of
money at all! You just wrote the right kind of a letter — and Santa Claus
did the rest! In that case he could have a car as well as Harold.

That night, when his early bedtime came, he handed his mother this letter
to read:

DEAR SANTA CLAUS Harold says you are going to bring him a Street-car. Wont you
please bring me one to. Not a little one but a Real one. I am trying hard to be a good boy,
and I want one very much.   DAVID DOUGLAS.

" Why, David," his mother said, " I thought you had given up the idea
of having a street-car."

" Yes, mama, I had; but you see this is different! "

" Different? "

" Of course! Don't you see? " he explained joyously. " If Santa Claus
brings it, it won't cost us any money at all — not even a cent! What makes
you look so sad? Don't you want me to have a car — even if Santa Claus
brings it? "

" Yes, dear, of course I would like to see you have one, but — "

" But what, mama? "

" David, if children ask *too* much, Santa Claus must disappoint them."

6

"Why?"

"Oh, for many reasons. You know mama has to say 'no' sometimes, much as she dislikes it."

He began to look troubled; then, suddenly recalling Harold's assurance, he took heart and said: "Harold's grandpapa told him if he wrote and asked Santa Claus for a car, he would get it—if he was a good boy; and I 'm sure if he brings Harold one, he will give me one too; please let me ask him!"

"Will you promise not to be unhappy if it does n't come after all?"

Oh, yes! He could promise that with a light heart. And next day the letter, laboriously copied in ink, with high-headed *h*'s and short-tailed *g*'s, was posted at "Harold's house" in a funny little Dutch house on the library-table. "Santa Claus comes down the chimbly and gets them," Harold explained. After that David's hopes ran sometimes high — sometimes low. In the latter state of mind he put the matter before Santa Claus again and again with such entreaties and promises as desperate longing suggested. Here are some of the letters Santa Claus found in the little Dutch house:

DEAR SANTA CLAUS Mama says a Street-car is too much, but I do want it so much, and I 'll be better than I ever was if you will please bring me one. DAVID.

DEAR SANTA CLAUS You need n't bring me a Bob-sled if you will only give me a Car. I can use my old sled till next Christmas. DAVID DOUGLAS.
P S I will do without the Fireman's Helmet. D. D.

DEAR SANTA CLAUS Please do bring me a Street-car. If I had a Car I would n't need a hook and Ladder wagon. I will be very careful of it. Mama says I am a good boy. DAVID DOUGLAS.

DEAR SANTA CLAUS Mama says I must n't expect a Street-car. But I want it more than Skates or Anything. If it is to much to ask for — please do bring it anyway — and I will give up the Skates, and the Police-patrol, and everything. You can keep the gun to.
Your loving DAVID DOUGLAS.
P S Even if it was a little broken in some places it would do. I could mend it. I 've got a hammer and some nails. I pounded them out strate. I hope you will. Please leave it in our side yard. Good by. DAVID DOUGLAS.

CHRISTMAS morning David woke early; every one else was fast asleep. His windows looked out on the side yard; if he had a car it was there now. That thought was too much for him. He slid out of bed and ran to the window; he had but to raise the shade; his heart was beating so hard he could fairly hear it, and he almost made a little petition with his lips as he put out his hand. One touch — it was up! He looked out upon a smooth, shining surface of snow. There was no car! The disappointment was too terribly desolating; he drew down the shade and crept back into bed, and there, since it was dark and no one would know, he shed a few hot, unhappy tears, fighting all the time against them, and never made a sound, although he could have sobbed aloud. He remembered his mother and his promise. Then, at last, he wondered if Harold had been disappointed too. The more he thought of it the more likely it appeared. He wished Harold no ill luck - but if there had been no distribution of cars whatever, it would alter the case considerably: it would be as though he had reached for the moon. He

"THERE STOOD A STREET-CAR LARGE AS LIFE!"

began to make the best of it, and to wonder what Santa Claus had left in his stocking, so that later, when he came down-stairs, and his father swung him up to kiss him good morning, saying, "Santa Claus slipped up on that car business, David,— must be he had no cars this year,— but your stocking looks pretty lumpy and tight," David was able to smile quite cheerfully. A Christmas stocking is a Christmas stocking, after all — mysterious and exciting, whatever your joys or sorrows. To Jack the queer shape was matter for suspicion, to be defied and barked at, as it divulged one secret after another; and when David tried on a fireman's helmet and new skates, with a lot of lesser treasures scattered all about, Christmas seemed pretty cheery.

Breakfast over, he and Jack set out, according to previous agreement, to see what Harold had in his Christmas stocking. They went in by the carriageway. Just as they took the first turn in the drive, David's heart gave a great jump and then stood still. Through the leafless lilac-bushes he could see a great yellow-and-white street-car in the midst of a sea of snow. It was a beautiful, heart-breaking vision; and there was Harold in brown reefer, leather cap, and leggings, leaning out of the car, shouting, "Hello, David! Hurry up! this car is just ready to start — hurry! You see," he cried triumphantly, as David waded through the snow, "I told you Santa Claus was goin' to bring me this car — why don't you get in?"

David stood mute beside the step, stroking Jack's head. Then for the first time the little boy remembered that David had had hopes too.

"Did you get a car?" he asked.

David's eyes filled; he tried to smile, but he could not speak, and he only shook his head as he looked from Harold to Ellen, Harold's sister. It was seldom Harold had to think of any one but himself, but he had a kind heart, and now he bestirred himself to make David happy. He let him work the change-slide and the doors, and gave him all coveted privileges. Then they went indoors to see the Christmas-tree; the candles were lighted and all the wonderful new toys displayed for David's benefit. There was something on the tree for David, too. He flushed with pleasure and wonder when Harold's grandpapa handed down books, candy, and a dark-lantern, saying, with a twinkle in his eye, "Queer, these things were left here by mistake, David! Santa Claus must walk in his sleep."

But an hour or two later, as David went home, he was thinking that the ways of Santa Claus were very strange. His whole soul had been set upon a street-car; he was ready to give up everything else to have that one joy. Now Harold merely asked for that along with a lot of other new pleasures. Yet Santa Claus brought a car to Harold, and to David none. It was matter to try the stoutest heart. Yet he was not envious. He had pluck and good sense, and he felt somehow that he ought to be as happy as he could; he tried to think about his skates and fireman's helmet. After all, a street-car was a tremendous gift to ask, even of Santa Claus. He had realized when he stood beside that dear car that it was a good deal even for Harold, and Harold had so many treasures it was not easy to surpass them. The dark-lantern swung in his hand; it was a comfort, and he felt dimly that in a day or two he would play burglar and policeman with great effect; but it could n't keep away a very choking feeling in his throat when he remembered Harold winding up the brake. As he came around the corner near home, with eyes fixed upon the slippery, trodden path, he had almost reached the house before he noticed that a part of the fence was down and wagon-wheels had cut the frozen crust of snow going through this opening into their yard. Before he could be surprised at this he came in full view of — what do you think? — a broad, strong truck, two strong gray horses

"WE 'LL HAVE TO LET THAT STRAP OUT A LITTLE, DRIVER, TILL YOU GET A TALLER CONDUCTOR," SAID HIS FATHER.

with heads down, looking at him from their soft eyes, and blowing a little at the snow; four or five men standing about, and — well, of course you 've guessed it! There stood a street-car large as life; a beautiful yellow-and-white car with " No. 11 " in gold figures on the side. A misty feeling swam before his eyes, through which the car seemed a beautiful dream that somehow had men in rough overcoats, gray horses, all strangely woven in it, as well as his mother, smiling and holding her hands tight together, watching him. Then somebody said, " Well, sir, how do you like it? " and David went forward with feet that hurried and yet seemed slow, — exactly like feet in a dream, — and somebody swung him up over the dash-board to the front platform and said, " Let me off at 116th Street, please, driver." And he found a big white placard hanging to the front brake, very neatly printed in black. David could spell out the words. They said, " For David Douglas from Santa Claus." And then David really came back to earth. He laughed and kissed his mother, and held his father's hand in both his own; he walked back and forth in the car, and took note of the familiar signs about no smoking and beware of pickpockets, and to use none but Quigley's Baking Powder. There was the cash-box and the brass slide for change in the front door. The brake worked, and the bell-strap rang a real bell when his father held him up to reach it. " We 'll have to let that strap out a little, driver, till you get a taller conductor." Well, it was perfect! — surpassing all dreams of joy and Christmas. Indeed, a bit of Christmas cheer had fallen to those rough-coated men who worked on Christmas day, for they were drinking coffee and eating gingerbread, and had cigars to smoke; even the horses, David noticed through his joy, had each an apple to eat. And Jack — Jack lost his head completely, and barked, and jumped on everybody with his snowy feet, and finally just tore round and round in a circle like mad.

Suddenly David's mother said, " Where is the letter, Tom? — did n't he give you a letter? "

" To be sure! I almost forgot the letter — let me see — here it is in this pocket "; and his father tore it open and began to read:

" MY DEAR DOUGLAS: I have taken the liberty of asking Santa Claus to deliver one of our old cars on your premises. I was growing rusty, but Santa Claus has waked me up by showing me a one-sided correspondence he 's been having with a young man by the name of David. I suddenly realized what a world of fun there was in Christmas, if you only knew how to get hold of it by the handle, as my grandfather used to say. I hope you and Mrs. Douglas will forgive me for getting my pleasure first and asking permission afterward. But when a man takes a holiday I suppose he may be allowed to take it in his own way. So please put this street-car into David's stocking! And I think this may not be a bad occasion for saying I 've never forgotten the time your mother made Christmas in my heart when I was a poor youngster with scarcely a stocking to hang. God bless you ! You have a fine boy.

"Very truly yours,   JOHN MILLER.

"P. S. That correspondence is a confidential matter between Santa Claus and me. No questions answered at this office.   J. M."

David wondered why his mother, who had been reading the letter over his father's arm, turned suddenly, while she was smiling, and cried on his father's shoulder.

The Tardy Santa Claus

BY KATE DOUGLAS WIGGIN

I AM a little Santa Claus
  Who somehow got belated;
My reindeer did n't come in time,
  And so of course I waited.
I found your chimneys plastered tight,
  Your stockings put away,

I heard you talking of the gifts
  You had on Christmas day;
So will you please to take me in
  And keep me till November?
I 'd rather start Thanksgiving day
  Than miss you *next* December!

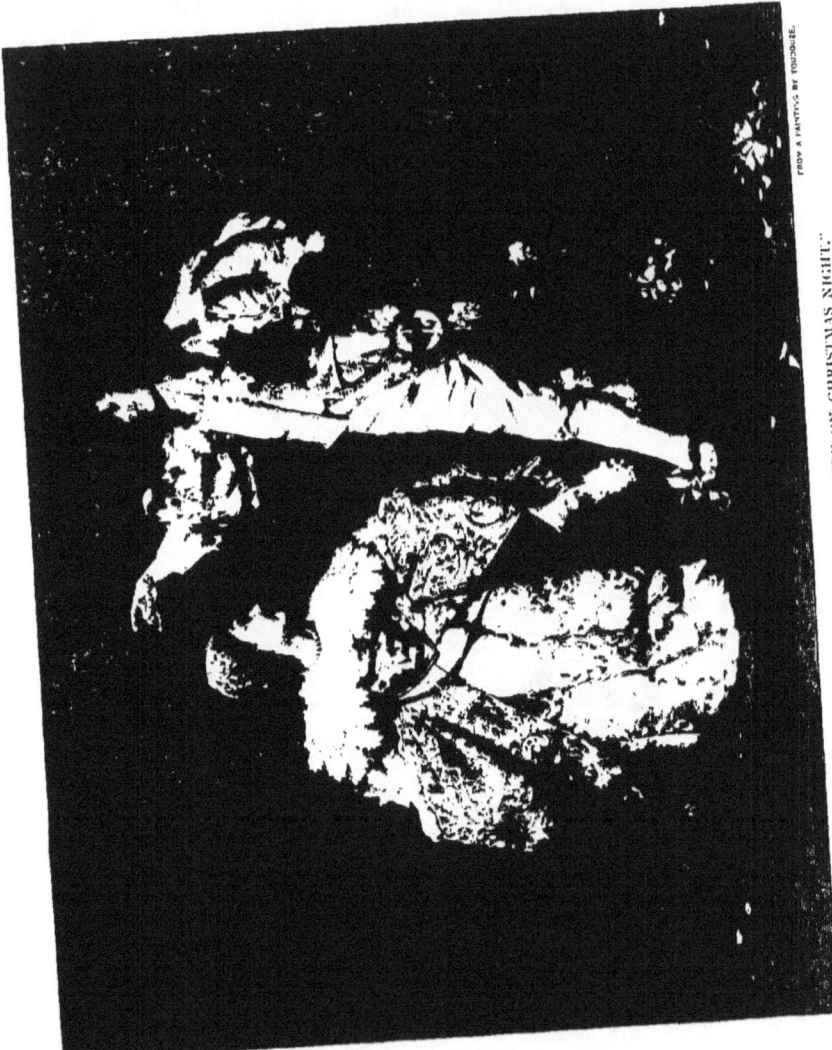

"AS THEY DANCED THEM A MEASURE ON CHRISTMAS NIGHT."

The Picture

BY MARY MAPES DODGE

 A LITTLE lady, a very young knight,—
Just a girl and a boy in each other's sight,—
Oh, their smiling faces were clear and bright,
Their velvets and satins with gems bedight!
Gold and laces and pearls had she,
And he was superb as a lad could be.
Their cheeks were rosy, their hearts were light,
As they danced them a measure on Christmas night.

'T was: "Ah, my lady!" and "Yea, my lord!"
And he touched as lightly his jeweled sword
As if 't were a flower; yet he knew with pride
The trick of the weapon that decked his side.
And she — why, the very sweep of her gown
Told how, in valor and grand renown
From sire to son, through court and crown,
The name she bore had been handed down!

And what was her name? And who was the boy? —
The two who danced in their stately joy.
I do not know, and I hardly care —
Their story is neither here nor there.
For girls and boys, young, merry, and fair,
Gladden our firesides everywhere.
They thrive and flourish to-day, as then —
The little ladies, the little men!
And, grand or humble, their hearts are light
When they tread them a measure on Christmas night.

The Elfin Bough.

BY HELEN GRAY CONE

THE little lad was grave and good;
  He ne'er had had such thoughts before.
(It happened in an English wood,
  Two hundred years ago, and more —
    Two hundred and twoscore.)

A sturdy little lad was he,
  Who always meant to do the right.
(His name was Year-of-Jubilee;
  His clear gray eyes first saw the light
    The year of Naseby fight.)

Along the woodland path he went
  Upon his errand, trudging slow;
His looks upon the ground were bent.
  Between the trunks the sunset glow
    Shone red across the snow.

It was the eve of Christmas day,
  When rigid rules aside were cast
By such as walked the wicked way:
  His sober household kept a fast;
    He wished the day were past!

In solemn fast small joy he had,
  Though shamed he was his thought to
    speak —
This little, hearty, hungry lad!
  Like ripened apple was his cheek,
    So round, and plump, and sleek.

Hark! what was that? He starts, he stops.
  The flutter of a rising bird?
A rabbit rustling in the copse?
  A stiff, sad-colored leaf that stirred?
    What was the sound he heard?

The light was round her as she stood,
  The slender maid, so wonder-fair,
In gown of green, and velvet hood.
  He felt a fear to see her there,
    So lonely and so rare!

She fixed her starry gaze on him,
  "I prithee now, good lad," said she,
"Canst break the bough with berries dim
  That springs so high on yonder tree?"
    "Yea, verily!" cried he.

In haste to serve so fair a maid,
  He plucked her down the elfin bough;
But once again he waxed afraid.
  With beating heart, with frowning brows
    He cried, "What maid art thou?"

"I doubt it is a heathen thing —
  My Aunt Refrain hath told me that.
Its leaf is like a leathern wing;
  It is as gruesome as a bat,
    A toad, or brindled cat!"

("Perchance she is a blue-eyed witch
  That dwelleth in the wood," he thought.
"Her silken gown is strange and rich.
  In subtle snare she hath me caught;
    My ruin, sure, is wrought!")

"Good Master Roundhead, shrink not so!"
  She said. "Thou wast a friend in need
To pluck my pearly mistletoe.
  A merry Christmas be thy meed
    For that most gentle deed!

"But merry Christmas is no more
  In English land! I mind me how
We kept the joyful feast of yore,
  In yon old ivied Hall, whence now
    I 've stolen to seek this bough!

"The men and maids, a rosy crowd,
  Made noisy mirth, and thought no sin.
With pipe, and tabor beating loud —
  Ah me, with what a joyous din
    They brought the Yule block in!

"On high the elfin bough would hang;
    And surely 't was a gleeful game,
And all the walls with laughter rang
    When Hodge kissed Moll beneath the
        same,
    Nor thought the jest a shame!

"With plums, and spice, and citron sweet,
    Madge cook would work in cunning wise;
She kneaded paste, she shredded meat —
    I trow thou wouldst have oped thine eyes
    To see the Christmas pies!

"Good store, good cheer, for many a
        year
    In that old Hall had we," she said;
"But now the days are grim and drear,
    The larder 's bare, and mirth is dead."
    She sighed, she turned, she fled.

Along the woodland path she went
    As swiftly as the speeding doe;
For now the wintry day was spent,
    Between the trunks the sunset glow
    Grew faint upon the snow.

And little Year-of-Jubilee
    Stood still, and stared, and heaved a sigh.
He thought, "Perhaps it would not be
    A grievous sin to wish that I
    Could *dream* of Christmas pie!"

Christmas in Bethlehem

BY EDWIN S. WALLACE

URING the Christmas season, when the thoughts of the civilized world turn to Bethlehem, many will wonder how the people there keep this greatest religious holiday. Very few American children can ever visit the little city among the Judean hills. Yet a number of travelers from America and Europe come to the Holy Land every year, to be among those who on Christmas day crowd the streets of the little city nestled among its fig-trees and olive-orchards.

It is a little city, and it does not take many people to crowd it; but, besides being the birthplace of Jesus, it is the birthplace of Israel's great warrior-king, David.

Bethlehem to-day has barely eight thousand inhabitants, and in appearance is not attractive. The streets are too narrow for vehicles; in fact, there is but one street in the town wide enough for carriages, and it is so very narrow that they cannot pass each other in it. The streets were made for foot travelers, donkeys, and camels.

Bethlehem is about five miles south of Jerusalem. Leaving the larger city by the Jaffa Gate, we take a carriage and ride rapidly over the fine road built but a few years ago. The carriage we are in and those we meet are wretched affairs. The horses are to be pitied, first, because they are not well cared for, and second, because their drivers are regular Jehus who drive them "furiously" up hill and down. In less than an hour we are in the market-place of Bethlehem, in front of the Church of the Nativity.

Let us suppose we have arrived on Christmas eve, in time to wander about and to become acquainted with the little city.

Of course it has changed in appearance since the time of the birth of Christ. It is larger, and better built. Now, as then, the houses are of stone, and, as cities and customs change but little in the East, we may safely infer that modern Bethlehem houses are much like those of nineteen hundred years ago. Perhaps some of the old buildings that were in existence so long ago may still be standing. Of course the great Church of the

Nativity was not then erected, nor were any of the large religious buildings we see. These are the memorials of a later date, built in honor of Him whose earthly life began here. One would have to be unmindful of his surroundings and very unimaginative not to wonder what the place was like on that night the anniversary of which we are celebrating.

We know that then, as on this December 24, it was filled with people.

VIEW OF BETHLEHEM. THE BUILDING ON THE LEFT IS THE CHURCH OF THE NATIVITY.

But those people had come for a different purpose. Augustus Cæsar, the master of the then known world, had issued an imperial decree ordering a general registration of all his subjects. This was for the purpose of revising or completing the tax-lists. According to Roman law, people were to register in their own cities — that is, the city in which they lived, or to which their village or town was attached. According to Jewish methods they would register by tribes, families, and the houses of their fathers. Joseph and Mary were Jews, and conformed to the Jewish custom. It was well known that he and Mary were of the tribe of Judah and family of David, and that Bethlehem was their ancestral home. Accordingly, they left the Nazareth home, in the territory of Zebulun, and came to David's "own city," in the territory of Judah.

They came down the east bank of the Jordan, crossed the river at Jericho, and came up among the Judean hills and valleys till they reached Bethlehem. It was a long journey, and a wearisome one; and, on arriving, a place of rest was the first thing they sought.

Evidently they had no friends living in the place; or, if they had, their houses were already filled. It was necessary that shelter be had, and immediately. In the khan, or inn, there was no room; so there was nothing to do but occupy a part of the space provided for cattle. It was not an unusual thing to do, and is often done to-day in these Eastern villages. In fact, they were about as comfortable there as in any khan. At a khan one may procure a cup of coffee and a place to lie down on the floor; but each guest provides his own bed and covering. This was all Joseph and Mary could have obtained in the inn, had there been room for them. And here in Bethlehem, in a stable, or a cave used for stabling animals, Jesus was born, and Mary "wrapped him in swaddling-clothes, and laid him in a manger."

A THRONG OF PILGRIMS ENTERING BETHLEHEM ON CHRISTMAS DAY.

A NEARER VIEW OF THE CHURCH OF THE NATIVITY.

There is one short walk we should take before entering the Church of the Nativity and the cave beneath it. This is to the Field of the Shepherds, about a mile east of the church, and the traditional place where the shepherds were watching their flocks on that momentous night. This may not be the exact place where the angels appeared, but there is no reason why we may not accept the tradition which has placed the event here. It has often been wondered why the shepherds had their flocks out all night in the winter-time; and the wonder is easily satisfied when we know that these were not ordinary flocks of sheep nor ordinary shepherds. These flocks were those specially selected for sacrifice in the Temple at Jerusalem, at the great Passover season, and were kept in the fields all the year. The shepherds were specially appointed.

Some time during that winter night the shepherds were dazzled by a light more brilliant than the stars, and roused by voices not of earth. The Christ, whose future sacrifice their flocks were to symbolize, was born; and

the angels were singing the good tidings. These shepherds were the first to hear and to spread the marvelous news.

Because of the event the angels were heralding, men have built the great Church of the Nativity in Bethlehem, and, indeed, all the great Christian churches and cathedrals of the world. It is because of this that people from every country in Europe and America will join the throng of native Christians in the "City of the Nativity," and rejoice in memory of the angels' song. It is because of this that there is to-day so much of "peace on earth" and "good will toward men."

And now we return in time to see the procession of bishops, priests, and people that is forming in the square in front of the church. Each is dressed in his most gorgeous robes. Turkish soldiers line both sides of the street to keep the way open for the procession to pass. The Latin Patriarch of Jerusalem has just arrived. The procession of priests, carrying banners and immense candles, meets him, then turns, and all go into the Latin Chapel through the main entrance. Following, we are surprised to find the main entrance so small. It can admit but one at a time, and that one must stoop to enter. From the masonry it can be seen that the entrance was once much larger. The reason for the change was that the Mohammedans at one time did all in their power to injure and annoy the Christians, and even used to ride on horseback into the very church. The door therefore was made small to protect the church from this sacrilege.

Once inside, we see we are in a very ancient structure. Part of the masonry dates from the time of Constantine, who built a magnificent basilica on this site, about the year 330 of our era. All we can see of the oldest work, however, probably dates from not later than Justinian's time, about 550 A. D. In any case, the church is a venerable building, and it has witnessed some stirring scenes. In it Baldwin the Crusader was crowned King of Jerusalem. It has been repaired a number of times; and once, when it needed a new roof, King Edward IV of England gave the lead to make one. This was about the year 1482. The lead roof did good service for about

two hundred years, and might have lasted much longer had not the Mohammedans melted it up to make bullets. However, another roof was soon
provided.

Inside, the building consists of a nave and double aisles. The aisles are
separated by two rows of columns made of red limestone. These columns
have plain bases, and are surmounted by Corinthian capitals. They are
nineteen feet high, and at the top of each a cross is engraved. The church is now owned by the Latin, Greek, and Armenian Christians.

THE GROTTO OF THE MANGER

Religious services will be held all night in the Latin Chapel of St. Catherine. At midnight a solemn mass will be said by the Patriarch of Jerusalem. The chapel is full of people, many of whom are sitting on the floor.

Before the procession descends into the Grotto of the Nativity we make our way there, so as to have a better view.

Originally it was simply a natural cave in the limestone rock. Now little of the native rock is seen. Marble slabs
cover the floor and line the walls. The ceiling, which is about ten feet high,
is resplendent with thirty-two brass lamps. Their light enables us to ex-
amine the many pictures, portraying scenes in the life of Jesus, which the
devotion of Christians has hung about the walls; but these pictures are
generally very poor as specimens of art. At the east end of the cave there
is a small recess in the rock, before which hang fifteen lamps. In the floor
of this recess a bright silver star is inlaid; it is nearly all worn away by
the constant kissing it receives. Around the star is an inscription in Latin,
which tells us that "Here, of the Virgin Mary, Jesus Christ was born."

Turning just a little to the right from this Place of the Star, and descending a few steps, we are in a small chamber called the Grotto of the Manger. The original manger is, of course, not here; it probably never was preserved, and many stories about it are inventions of a much later date. Here, also, is a little altar on the place where the Wise Men from the East prostrated themselves before the infant Jesus. These three — the places of the birth, the manger, and the adoration — are all in what is called the Chapel of the Nativity.

Passing out of this chapel by the steps leading into the Greek Church of St. Mary, we are again in the streets of Bethlehem.

It is a relief to get away from the glare of lamps, the smoke of candles, and the heavy odors of burning incense, and to breathe again the fresh air blowing over the Judean hills. The streets are very quiet, for all not in the church have retired to their homes. Occasionally people leave the church, and are driven away in their carriages to Jerusalem, though most visitors

E. CHAPEL OF THE NATIVITY

remain all night. We can wander through the streets and over the neighboring hills, for the clear moon makes it almost as bright as day.

How peaceful it all is! Indeed, it seems a most suitable place for the coming to the world of "the Prince of Peace."

Faint streaks of the dawn are beginning to show in the sky above the hills of Moab. Rapidly they grow longer and brighter, and soon it is daybreak, and we know that it is Christmas in Bethlehem.

But we miss much of the accustomed joy of the day. At home there would be good cheer, the companionship of loved ones, and the giving and receiving of gifts. Here there is little of this, the home life of the people is so different from ours. Christmas day in Bethlehem is not the Christmas day we know; it is full of religious ceremonies, and when these are over young and old go back to their accustomed life. The faces of the boys and girls I saw in Bethlehem last Christmas were not such faces as I should have seen in any city or village in America. And I knew the reason. It was because Christmas to them was much the same as any other day of the year. And so it requires more than Bethlehem to make Christmas what we like to have it. It requires loving home life and the presence of the spirit of the Christ Child in the heart. And yet, who would not be glad to spend one Christmas eve and day where He who made the glad day possible was born?

Misplaced Confidence

BY FLORENCE E. PRATT

WILLY in the corner crying! What can be the matter?
What can ail my happy little, merry little boy?
Tears on Christmas morning! — tell us what 's the trouble.
Who has caused the tears that spoil our little darling's joy?

"Grandpa 's gone a-skating with the little skates I gave him;
Aunty 's sitting reading in the fairy-book I bought;
Mama 's playing horses with that pair of reins — a present
I made to her last Friday. It 's mean! because I thought —

"Boohoo! — I thought that grandpa was a gen'rous sort of grandpa,
And I thought that all the rest of 'em were generous, you see;
And after they had all admired the pretty things I gave them,
They 'd think such things more suit'ble for a little boy like me!"

"The Christmas Inn"

BY ELLA F. MOSBY

ONG ago, in one of England's old shires there was a famous hostelry know as "The Saracen's Head," and on the creaking sign-board was painted a fearful paynim with gleaming white teeth and frowning eyebrows. But one day it became "The Christmas Inn," with the genial device of a sprig of holly promising good cheer and a jolly welcome. To tell the reason of the inn's change of name will be to give a page out of the obscure chronicles of the common lives of men, women, and children more than three centuries ago. But the quaint, sweet incident is well worth calling to mind at the blessed Christmas season.

It is found briefly set down between items of household expenses, and statements of journeys to London and back, and records of deaths in battle, and costs of trials for treason, in the household books of the worshipful families of the Hightowers and the Barnstaples in the years from 1461 to 1483. It comes like a little flute's silvery tune between the blare of trumpets and the clash and clang of swords in those rough days, and is so briefly told that I shall have to piece it out for you in my own way.

It was Christmas eve in 1465, and snow had fallen thick and fast, covering from sight the charred and blackened gable-ends of many a ruined or desolate house. There had been hard fighting in old England, "merry" no longer when class fought against class, section against section, people against nobles, east against west, and when friend and kinsman were at deadly feud; when the white rose of York and the red rose of Lancaster were in conflict for the English throne. But, for the sacred Christmas season, a truce had been agreed upon, and for thirty days there would be no blow struck.

The Saracen's Head looked fierce and grim in the wild wind and drifting snow; but mine host of the inn, Thomas Curdy, came to the door and gazed up and down the highroad with a broad, red, jolly face of hospitality and welcome. It was so wild a storm that he was about to shut and bar the great door earlier than was usual; but he would fain catch some sign of approaching travelers, man and beast, before doing so.

"No traveler abroad to-night!" quoth he, with a sigh of regret, as he went back within the red, glowing circle of warmth thrown out by the huge Yule logs of the blazing fire, and rubbed his stout hands before its leaping flames.

"Marry, then, this blessed eve there will be no drinking nor brawling here, nor quarreling in men's cups till they come to blows, truce or no truce!" answered Dame Curdy, contentedly, her rosy, motherly face and fat figure seeming to shed in its way as much comfort around her as did the fire.

A jolly pair they were, and to see how the flames made them ruddier and jollier and cheerier every moment was a sight for Christmas eve. The Hightowers and Barnstaples chronicles have little to say of this honest pair, but nevertheless they are quite as worthy our attention as any Lancastrian Hightowers or Yorkist Barnstaples of them all.

"Travel, good dame, travel up and down the highroad brings good luck to the Saracen's Head, and it 's a bad night that stops it!"

"Aye, I wot — travel in peace. But no bands of fighting-men, to give the honest house a hard name — and no reckonings paid either. But in this storm, I warrant, none will stir abroad that can bide at home, not even your thirsty cronies from the village, Hobbs and Giles."

"An' if a storm stops them —" But here a loud, shrill blast from a trumpet sounded keen and clear across the wild wind.

Mine host started up, alert and ready, and Dame Curdy wrung her hands in dismay.

"More fighting-men, alack! I hear the wringing of their armor now as they ride through the gate. May the saints keep watch and ward over us poor sinners, for that is none other than Sir John Keightley's call! They are all the Earl's men."

The good landlady loved peace, and hated war, and her kindly heart dreaded the turbulent scenes that old kitchen had often witnessed; but her lamentations were to no purpose, as she well knew. Of all people they dared not offend the redoubtable Earl of Hightowers, or any of his stout men-at-arms.

In a few seconds the inn was full of bustle and confusion. Hostlers ran, maids hurried here and there; and while the dame gave shrill orders in the kitchen, Thomas Curdy shouted a welcome through the fierce blasts of wind that drove the whirling snow through the wide-open doors.

Across the threshold — with wind and snowflakes — entered the late comers: Sir John Keightley, a weather-beaten, rugged, and scarred old vet-

eran of many a hard-fought fight, and at least nine or ten stout men with
him, roughly dressed, and armed with the longbow, as were most of the
common soldiers at that time.   But as they came out of the night and the
storm into the circle of light around the great hearth, Thomas Curdy saw
that this was no ordinary band of fighting-men.   There were women — three

"ACROSS THE THRESHOLD ENTERED THE LATE COMERS"

of them, and one who carried herself so haughtily that mine host, who was
used to the ways of great people, shrewdly suspected that she was no more
than some great lady's attendant; for he had always noticed that the great
lady herself was likely to be more simple and quiet in her ways than her maid.
    And Sir John Keightley carried in his arms a bundle which he would let
no one touch, but strode ahead in front of the great fire, and, kneeling down,
began tenderly to unfasten wrap after wrap.   What a hush of amazement at

first, and then what exclamations of wonder and delight from Dame Curdy and her women when the last wrapping was thrown off, and out stepped the daintiest little girl ever seen! She was but two years and six months old; and she laughed out merrily like the ripple of water or the singing of the early winds in spring through the young leaves; and looking up at the big knight, with tiny hands she began to brush the snowflakes from the grizzled hair and beard of the old soldier.

"Who is this dear heart?" cried Dame Curdy; and a clear little flute-like voice answered in the softest of tones:

"I'm Lady Margery" (or "Marg'y," as she pronounced it)—"Rosamond Vere."

Her hair was of reddish gold of the finest silken texture. It was cut square across her brow in front, and hung over her lace frill behind. Her eyes were of a velvety black-blue color, and had a look of wistful tenderness that was contradicted by the laughing, mischievous mouth and the dimples that lurked in cheek and chin. That look must have come from the young mother who died not long after the husband, only son of the Earl of Hightowers, was cut down in a skirmish with the Yorkists at Stapleton-on-the-Moor. The baby girl had her mother's eyes and her father's chin; but the likeness that delighted the portly landlady, and made her smile cheerily and rub her fat hands, was to little Margery's stately old grandmother, the countess, with her tall head-dress. For just at that time the fashionable gentlemen wore puffed and slashed doublets, and shoes ridiculously broad like hoofs; and fashionable ladies, like the countess, were adorned with head-dresses ornamented by projecting horns, and looked very grand, no doubt.

"Pretty lamb, how she favors the Countess herself with that proud turn of her sweet head!"

Dame Curdy was right. This baby, in her little rose-colored camlet gown, with the gold of her precious head for a crown, ordered her retainers about—Sir John most of all—more royally than the Earl dared to do. But it was, after all, a right heavenly rule of love, albeit a wilful one.

She would have none of her nurse when, after a dainty grace, she had eaten her supper of cream and fine white wheat bread; but she ran away, laughing so that she tripped and almost fell, past the men-at-arms to stout old Sir John Keightley, and climbed on his knee in triumph—for she was sure of having her own way there.

Sir John had been sent by the Earl to bring home his little granddaughter, too young to grieve over her double loss, and had fallen in love with the little maid from the first sound of her childish voice.

She prattled away merrily now, her silvery, piping tones sounding curiously sweet among the gruff voices of the rough soldiers. The men were watching with keen appetites the stirring of the savory dishes, as the landlady hung over the fire, every now and then glancing at the pretty child on the knight's knee.

"Hark! hark!" cried Margery, suddenly, making with her baby finger an imperative gesture for silence. "Marg'y hears the big horn coming!" and laughing out with delight, she doubled up her rosy fists and began to blow in pretty mimicry, her eyes shining like stars in her excitement. Then quickly changing, she clapped her tiny palms together, crying, "Kling-klang, kling-klang!"

They all heard now what the finer ear of the child had sooner detected — the trumpet-call coming nearer and nearer, and the clang of arms.

"Who think you that these may be, landlord?" asked Sir John, anxiously glancing at the golden head against his breast.

"I fear me it is Sir Joseph Barnstaples's men," answered mine host, deprecatingly, for the Barnstaples were Yorkists, and long at enmity with the Hightowers faction; and again the good dame sighed and wrung her hands in dismay.

Fearing some possible attack, in spite of the solemn proclamation of the truce, Sir John made his men resume their weapons while the big door was being unbarred.

Then what a sight! No such wonderful night had the old Saracen's Head ever known before. Here, again, with the soldiers were nurses — two nurses in russet kersey gowns, carrying each a small bundle; and out of these bundles, when unwrapped, appeared *two* babies, twin girls of eighteen months old! Sir Joseph Barnstaples's second son had married in one of the southern shires a rich heiress, who had died of a fever; and now, the grandame being dead also, the father was sending them, like the wee lady with Sir John, under military convoy back to his old home at Barnstaples Manor.

The women clapped their hands, and laughed with "Ohs!" and "Ahs!" and "Dear hearts!" — even the soldiers laughed — but nobody was so pleased as the little "Lady Marg'y," as she gazed, with wide-open eyes and crimson lips just parted by a smile and showing a few white pearls of teeth, at the demure twin babies.

Barbara and Janet Barnstaples, as the firelight danced over their little, smooth, round heads, darker than Margery's, could not be coaxed into a smile. Their four dark, grave eyes wondered solemnly at all the noise and all the strange faces, and the two little mouths were drawn up for a cry,

MARGERY AND THE TWINS AT "THE CHRISTMAS INN"

when all at once they caught sight of Margery, bending forward, and two faint little dimples showed for a moment, one on each right cheek. At least, Barbara smiled first, and then Janet followed suit.

THE snow came down thick and fast that night, but old Sir John, wont to dream of bugles sounding alarm, and of ambuscade and skirmish, dreamed of a long-forgotten meadow above the weir, where the blue speedwell grew and bloomed until the ground was all of a delicious blue like the angelic robes in the old chapel windows ; and waking next morning, cast about in his mind as to whether this might not betoken death ; for had he not heard all his life that

Flowers out of season

meant

Trouble out of reason?

It would seem very funny, nowadays, for an experienced and brave old gentleman to worry about dreams and signs, but people were not very wise about such things in the fifteenth century.

The same night, the old nurse was awakened by a light footfall in the room, and, peeping out from the bedclothes, saw a flitting white figure cross the dusky space that was but dimly lighted by the gleams from the dying embers.

She put her hand out for her nursling. The little nest in the bed was warm, but empty. Up she started in alarm, and saw — a sight for fairyland ! For little Margery, hearing one of the twin babies cry in her sleep, and her nurse not waking, had stolen out of bed and was busy tucking her in and cooing to her like a little wood-dove. The old nurse called her softly, and the little bare feet pattered across the floor to the bed, to be caught up and cuddled to sleep again.

The next morning Margery would not eat until the twins had been put one on each side of her at the table ; and then she would feed them, giving now Barbara a bit of the wheaten loaf, and now Janet a spoonful of cream. And if she ever gave to Janet first, Janet would shake her small head, as brown and glossy as a nut, and point with her wee finger to Barbara. The whole party were in high glee, until Margery noticed with displeasure that too many were looking on. For the very hostlers and the scullions had stolen to the doors to peep at the strange sight of three babies among all those soldiers, who now seemed to be quite friendly together, and wonderfully quiet in their innocent presence.

Margery turned her head quickly to Sir John, and asked, with an air that delighted the landlady, " Are dose folks all *so* hungry ? "

There was such a shout of applause that the intruders fled abashed, and the little lady gravely returned to her breakfast.

Very soon the two convoys went on their separate roads; and whether the little lady of Hightowers and the twin heiresses of Barnstaples ever met again, and were friends or foes, our chronicle does not say. But the coming of the three babies to the Saracen's Head on Christmas eve was not soon forgotten, and in memory of the day of good will that grim old Moslem was hauled down from his creaking sign-post, and in his place swung gaily to and fro a freshly painted holly branch with the words " THE CHRISTMAS INN " beneath it.

SANTA CLAUS: "AHA! CHILDREN ALL ASLEEP! THAT 'S WHAT I LIKE TO SEE!"

(A Dialogue to Introduce the Christmas-tree.)

BY EUDORA S. BUMSTEAD

CHARACTERS.

SANTA CLAUS. A man with long white hair and beard, coat and cap of fur.

1ST BOY.
 2D BOY.
 3D BOY. } Dressed in fancy uniforms, with plumed hats, sashes, and swords.

1ST GIRL.
 2D GIRL.
 3D GIRL. } Dressed as waiting-maids, in dark frocks and stockings, white aprons and caps; carrying trays.

The third boy and the third girl should be the smallest of the company, and the boy should be trained to speak in a very deliberate and emphatic manner, with an air of great importance.

SCENE. — A small stage, with a Christmas-tree curtained off, L. Stage curtain rises, discovering the six children grouped in a semicircle, fronting audience. Third boy at right, and third girl at left of the others.

1ST BOY.   This day has lasted 'most a week,
     I honestly believe.
1ST GIRL.   I think so too. But now, at last,
     It 's really Christmas eve.

2D BOY.   And we are here to guard the tree
     Till good Kriss Kringle comes.
2D GIRL.   And we are here to wait on him,
     And pass the sugar-plums.

3D BOY.   I 'spect by now the tree is full —
     Every tiny shoot.
I wish that Santa Claus were here, —
     We 'd — pick — the fruit.

3D GIRL.   What does make him stay so long?
     It must be getting late.
Come, let 's sing our Planting Song
     While we have to wait.

(ALL SING. Air: "Johnny Comes Marching Home.")
We 've planted a beautiful Christmas-tree,
    Hurrah! Hurrah!
Its branches are strong as strong can be,
    Hurrah! Hurrah!
But won't they bend with the fruitage fair
That good St. Nicholas makes them bear,
And we 'll all be so glad that we planted the
    Christmas-tree.

Our fathers and mothers are here to-night.
    Hurrah! Hurrah!
They 've come to see the wonderful sight,
    Hurrah! Hurrah!
We hope St. Nicholas won't forget,
Some fruit for them on the tree we 've set;
And we 'll all be so glad that we planted the
    Christmas-tree!

There 's lovely fruit in summer and fall,
But the Christmas crop is the best of all;
And we 'll all be so glad that we planted the
    Christmas-tree!

1ST GIRL.   There 's the tree we planted,
                Curtained out of sight.
1ST BOY.   Let us take a peep and see
                If everything is right.

(All tip-toe L. and peep cautiously behind the curtain.)

2D GIRL.   It 's rather dark, but, seems to me,
                There 's nothing to be seen.
3D BOY.   Nothing on the Christmas-tree?
                What — can it — mean!

3D GIRL.   Where are the nuts and candies?
2D BOY.   I can't see a crumb!

1ST GIRL.
Where 's Mr. Santa Claus?
1ST BOY.
Don't believe he 'll come!

2D GIRL.
What if he were frozen in,
Away up there?
3D BOY.
Or what if he were eaten
By a great — big — bear!

3D GIRL.
Or what if all his helpers
Were gone upon a strike!
3D BOY.
I tell you that 's a prospect
That I — don't — like!

1ST BOY.
Come, let 's go and find him.
Don't you think we might?
1ST GIRL.
It 's cold and dark outside, boys;
Don't you know it 's night?

2D BOY.
I tell you, we are soldiers,
Whom nothing ever scares.
3D BOY.
Wish we were with Santa Claus —
We 'd   kill — the bears!

We 'll serve St. Nicholas all we can,
    Hurrah! Hurrah!
And he shall be our nursery-man,
    Hurrah! Hurrah!

2D GIRL.   I wonder if his sleigh is caught
                With snow-drifts all about?
3D BOY.   I wish that we could find him;
                We 'd — dig — him out!

3D GIRL. Perhaps he has some reindeers
That are not the fleetest sort.

1ST BOY. I wish we were behind 'em:
We 'd have good sport.

3D BOY. I tell you, we are soldiers
Whom nothing ever scares;
If we could find our Santa Claus,
We 'd — kill — the bears!

3D GIRL. I 'm 'fraid you boys are braggarts.
But did you ever know
What happened at a Christmas-tree
A long time ago?

3D BOY. Oh, no! Let 's have the story!

1ST GIRL. We 'll all be very still.

1ST BOY. Tell us all about it, now.

3D GIRL. Well, then, I will.

Once there were three little boys.
They quarreled and they fought
Over all the pretty presents
That Santa Claus had brought.
And they never gave the smallest bit
Of anything they had
To any poorer little boy,
To try to make him glad.

At last they set a Christmas-tree,
For their three selves alone.
They meant that every speck of fruit
Should be their very own.
And when they lit the candles
They saw that great big tree
Was just as full of Christmas fruit
As ever it could be.

But just when they were ready
To gather all those things,
They heard the glass a-breaking
And a sudden rush of wings;
And right in through the window
Flew — what do you suppose?
You 'd never guess in all the world —
'T was three black crows! —
Big, black crows!

They perched around the Christmas-tree —
And there was no more joy —
With such a solemn, blaming look
They looked at every boy.

And those three boys just looked at them,
And did n't dare to stir,
Till all at once they flapped their wings —
Buzz! — Whizz! — Whir!
And right in sight of all those boys
They changed — as quick as scat!
In place of every solemn crow
Was a big black cat!
A fierce black cat!

They sat around the Christmas-tree
And there was no more joy;
With such a "scareful," hungry look
They gazed at every boy.
Those boys just shook and trembled,
And feared that they would fall,
For they knew they 'd all be eaten
If the cats were not so small.
Then, all at once, so sly and still,
It happened unawares,
Those dreadful cats had changed their
shapes
To three black bears!
Big BLACK BEARS!

(All look horrified. Noise behind the curtain near Christmas-tree.)

ALL THE BOYS.   What 's that?
ALL THE GIRLS. Shoo! Scat!

(During next speeches all retreat slowly backward to farthest corner.)

1ST GIRL. What can be in there?
3D BOY.   Oh, dear! I 'm most afraid
It might be a bear!

2D GIRL.   Look! look! There 's something
moving!
I see some fur! It 's gray!
1ST BOY.   I 'll watch this corner;
He sha'n't get away!

2D BOY.   Just let him come out boldly,
And fight us. if he dare!
3D BOY (faintly, pressing close to the wall).
Don't be frightened, any one;
We 'll — kill — the bear!

(Enter Santa Claus, L. Children gaze in astonishment till he speaks, then surround and cling to him.)

SANTA CLAUS.

Ho! Hullo! my little folks!
Looking out for bears?
'T is only one of Santa's jokes,
To catch you unawares.

Your love for what is true
    and right;
Your tender heart and
    smile so bright;
Your own dear self, with
    us to-night;
  Santa Claus, dear Santa
    Claus.

We 'll think about you all
    the year,
  Santa Claus, dear Santa
    Claus;
And often wish that you
    were here,
  Santa Claus, dear Santa
    Claus.
We 'll try our best to be
    like you,
In all our duties, kind and
    true;
As glad to share with
    others, too,
  Santa Claus, dear Santa
    Claus.

But now you 've turned
    the joke on me;
  You 've caught me, I 'll
    be bound!
Well, you shall help me
    strip the tree,
  And pass the fruit around.

3D BOY.

But first we 'll sing a little
    song,
  And every word is true;

(Takes Santa Claus' hand
and lays his cheek against it.)

Dear Mr. Santa Claus,
  We 'll – sing   for you.

(*All sing. Air:* "Maryland,
  my Maryland.")

We love you more than
    we can sing,
  Santa Claus, dear Santa
    Claus;
And not alone for what
    you bring,
  Santa Claus, dear Santa
    Claus.

SANTA CLAUS.

Now may joy and love and cheer
  Brighten all you see !
One good look, my children dear,
  Here 's your Christmas-tree !

(Instrumental music. Santa Claus withdraws the curtain from before the tree. Allow sufficient time for all to enjoy the sight of the ornamented tree, and then let the six children distribute the gifts as Santa Claus takes them from the tree.)

Molly Ryan's Christmas Eve

BY W. J. HENDERSON

T was bitter cold on the night before Christmas in latitude 40° 30' north, longitude 50° west. That lies just south of the southern extremity of the Grand Banks of Newfoundland, and a wild, melancholy, uneasy part of the Atlantic Ocean it is at the best of times. But on a Christmas eve, with the wind in the northwest, it is a home of desolation. The wind was northwesterly on that particular Christmas eve, and it was blowing what landsmen would call half a gale and a sailor a brisk breeze. But the good steamer *Astoria*, from Liverpool for New York, made no account of a wind which served only to increase the draft in her fire-room, and to enable the engineer to squeeze half a dozen more revolutions per minute out of the propeller. She was making a fair nineteen and a half knots per hour.

When the cold spray came over the weather-bow like a discharge of shot made of ice, and slashed the face of the first officer away up on the bridge, he only pulled his cap down more tightly over his ears, hauled the muffler higher around his neck, squinted at the compass-card, and gritted his teeth, for he realized that the mighty machine under his feet was letting the degrees of longitude drop astern at a pace which promised the steamship a splendid winter record.

"If the Captain had only laid the course to the nor'rard," he muttered, "we 'd 'a' broken the record. I don't see wot he 's a-buggaluggin' around here for as if we was in the middle o' summer, with ice on the Banks. Keep your eyes in the bowl, you!"

The last remark was addressed to the man at the wheel.

"I thought I seed summat w'en we riz to the last sea, sir," said the man.

"See! Ye could n't see your grandmother's ghost on sich a night, lad. It 's blacker 'n the inside o' a cuttlefish."

It was black, and no mistake. Little Molly Ryan, who was among the poor steerage passengers with her father and mother, wondered if the ship was sailing on the ocean or just on darkness. Molly ought not to have been on deck, and if any sailor had seen her she would have been quickly sent below. But she was such a little body, and she huddled up so closely under the edge of the poop, that no one discovered her. It was so gloomy and close in the steerage quarters, and so many poor women were sick, that Molly had stolen away, while her parents were dozing, to catch a breath of fresh air. The cold wind seemed to pierce through her, but she was fascinated by the darkness; and after a time she climbed up and sat on the rail, looking at the ghostly foam as it hurled itself against the iron side and swept hissing away under the quarter. Molly was in great danger, but she did not know it. She fancied she saw, away down there in the black-and-white waters, a beautiful Christmas-tree loaded with silver toys, that came and went with the foam. Molly had never had a Christmas-tree, but she had heard about them, and her fondest hope was that some day she might see one. She leaned far out, looking down into the waters, and, of course, she could not know how close the bark *Mary Ellis* was.

But the *Mary Ellis* was altogether too close. She was flying swiftly along, before the wind, thundering down into the yawning hollows that flung her bows aloft again with terrible force, and her course was diagonally across the bows of the steamer. Now the skipper of the *Mary Ellis* was a rough, mean man, and he was trying to save oil, so his side-lights were not burning. But those of the steamer were, and the watch on the bark's deck ought to have seen them. But for some reason they did not. So every moment, the two ships kept drawing closer and closer together, and just as a steward happened to catch sight of Molly, and called to her to get down, there was a sudden outbreak of shouts forward.

The first officer immediately called a swift order to the man at the wheel, then sprang to the engine-room telegraph, and signaled the engineer to stop.

A few seconds later there was a jar, a noise of rending wood, and the *Astoria* struck the *Mary Ellis* a glancing blow on her port quarter, carrying away a part of her bulwarks. At the same instant Molly Ryan fell off the *Astoria's* rail into the sea.

"Man overboard!" screamed the steward, who reached the spot just a moment too late to catch her.

But it takes a long time to stop a steamer going nearly twenty knots an hour, and by the time that the first boat was lowered the *Astoria* was far beyond the spot where Molly went over.

Fortunately for Molly, when she came to the surface half strangled, her little hands struck something hard which floated. With the strength of despair she climbed upon it. It was the part of the *Mary Ellis's* bulwarks knocked off in the collision. Still more fortunately for Molly, the captain of the bark, rushing on deck and hearing the cry, "Man overboard," thought that the words came from some one on his own vessel, and ordered one of his boats lowered away. Groping in the blackness amid the tumbling waters, the crew of this boat found Molly, and took her aboard the bark.

"THE TWO SHIPS KEPT DRAWING CLOSER AND CLOSER TOGETHER."

"Wot!" exclaimed the captain; "only a kid? Take her forward, some of you, an' see her looked after."

And having made sure that the bark was not seriously injured, he returned to his cabin to sleep.

"Wal, Han'some," said a long, lean seaman with a pointed beard, who looked for all the world like a Connecticut farmer, "wot ye goin' to dew with yer wrackage, now ye got her?"

"Thaw her out," said "Handsome," as he was called, carrying Molly into the galley.

The sailors fell into a general discussion as to how Molly should be treated, for the poor little thing was quite unconscious, and her clothes were freezing on her. However, after a while she was undressed, properly and gently "thawed out," and put to bed. The sailor called Handsome mixed a warm drink and poured it between her teeth. She gave a little gasp, opened her eyes, and gazed around.

"Oh," she muttered, "there is n't any Christmas-tree, after all."

And with that she fainted away again. The sailors looked at one another in solemn silence, till finally one said, in a deep bass voice:

"Well, if she hain't a-'untin' fer trees on the so'therly end o' the Grand Banks!"

"Wal, that 's wot she 's a-lookin' fur, an' that 's wot she 's a-goin' fur to get," said Handsome, slapping one huge fist into the other; and then he and the other seamen sat down under the forecastle lamp and conversed earnestly in low tones. After several minutes of talk they all arose, and Farmer Joe said:

"Han'some, yeou air consid'ble peert w'en yeou 're peert. But there's no time to lose. We must get to work right away."

While the rough sailors were at work, little Molly passed from a state of unconsciousness to one of sleep. The big seamen took turns in watching over her. It was not a pretty bedroom that Molly had that night. It was dark and dingy, and full of weird noises of groaning timbers. A swinging lantern threw changeful shadows into all the corners, and showed some very rude bunks in which several sailors off watch were trying to snatch a brief rest. Just behind those bunks against the stout sides of the bark the seas burst in booming shocks, and ever and anon there was a noise of falling water overhead. Up and away the bows would soar and then plunge down again with a sickening rush into the turmoil of foam. But of course the sailors thought nothing of all these things. The forecastle was their home, and they were long ago hardened to its sights and sounds. In spite of everything, Molly slept quite soundly, wrapped in a rough blanket and with a pea-jacket spread over her shoulders, while Handsome and the other sailors were at work with a boat-hook, some small pieces of wood, oakum, and green paint. Whatever it was that they were making, it was strange enough to look at; but their hearts were in their work, and they conversed earnestly in low tones. At last it was finished and set up in a bucket close against the bulkhead, where the lantern shed its fitful light full upon it.

"Werry good, too," said Handsome, gazing at it; "but it won't do unless it 's got somethin' onto it."

And then those sailor-men went rummaging in their chests, and as they had been voyagers in all parts of the globe, they brought forth some curious toys to put upon the wondrous Christmas-tree which they had made. Handsome contributed three large shells from the Indian Ocean, a dried mermaid, and a small Hindu god which answered very well for a dolly. Another produced a South African dagger, Chinese puzzle, and three brass nose-rings from a South Pacific island. Farmer Joe brought out a stuffed marmoset, an Indian amulet, and a tintype likeness of himself. A fourth sailor fished out of his chest a beautiful India-silk handkerchief and a string of coral. Handsome gravely hung them on the Christmas-tree. When all was done, he stepped back and studied the effect.

"Werry good, too," he said.

"Yas," said Farmer Joe; "I guess yeou could n't get any sech tree as that to haome."

At six o'clock on Christmas morning Molly awoke. It was still dark, and the lantern's light was but dim. The sailors were huddled back in the corner farthest from their wonderful Christmas-tree, which was set where the child's eyes were most likely to fall on it as soon as she sat up in her bunk. So when Molly awoke she did

HANDSOME'S CHRISTMAS-TREE.

sit up and stare straight in front of her with sleepy eyes, trying to collect her thoughts and make out where she was. Gradually she became conscious of the tree. Her eyes opened wider and wider. She almost ceased to breathe for a few moments. Then suddenly she clapped her hands together and, with a little scream of delight, cried joyously: "Why, it 's a Christmas-tree!"

The sailors nudged one another, and Handsome could not restrain a chuckle. Molly heard, and looked around at them. A puzzled expression came over her face, and she studied her surroundings for a minute.

"'IS N'T THAT A CHRISTMAS-TREE?' MOLLY ASKED."

"Is n't that a Christmas-tree?" she asked.

"That 's wot it is!" cried English; "an' we also is Santa Clauses."

"Oh!" exclaimed Molly; "what funny Santa Clauses! I always thought there was only one."

"Well, aboard this 'ere bark there is several."

"And oh!" cried Molly, clapping her hands and jumping out of the bunk, "what a lot of funny things I 've got for my Christmas! I never got

much before. But I think I 'd rather have my father and mother, please."
And then she looked as if she were about to cry.

"Don't go fer to cry," said Handsome, "an' I 'll sing ye a song."

"Oh, you *are* a nice Santa Claus!" cried Molly, brightening up.

"All the rest o' you Santa Clauses jine in the chor-i-us," said Handsome,
standing up and taking a hitch at his trousers. Then he sang:

Oh, the cook he 's at the binnacle,
   The captain 's in the galley,
An' the mate he 's at the foretop,
   Wi' Sally in our alley;
An' the steward 's on the bobstay,
   A-fishin' hard fer sole;
The wind is up an' down the mast;
   So roll, boys, roll.

"CHOR-I-US"

Roll, boys, roll, boys!
   Never mind the weather.
No matter how the wind blows,
   We 'll all get there together.

Oh, the captain could n't steer a ship,
   Because he was a Lascar;
The cook he had to show the way
   From France to Madagascar;
The ship she could n't carry sail,
   Because she had no riggin';
The crew they had to live on clams —
   'T was werry deep fer diggin'.

Roll, boys, roll, boys! etc.

The cook says: "Let the anchors go!"
   The crew says: "We ain't got 'em."
The captain yells: "Then pack your trunks!
   We 'll all go to the bottom."
The steward hove the lead, sir;
   'T was three feet deep, no more;
So every mother's son of us
   Got up and walked ashore.

Roll, boys, roll, boys! etc.

The land was full o' cannibals,
   W'ich made it interestin'.
We told 'em not to eat us, fer
   We was sich bad digestin'.
The king comes down to see us,
   An' he sports a paper collar;
An' he says if we 'll clear out o' that
   He 'll give us half a dollar.

Roll, boys, roll, boys! etc.

So we fells an injy rubber-tree,
   An' makes a big canoe,
About the shape and pattern
   Of a number twenty shoe:
The cook he draws a sextant,
   An' the captain draws his pistol:
One shoots the sun, an' one the king,
   An' off we goes fer Bristol.

Roll, boys, roll, boys, etc.

An' now we 're safe ashore again,
   We 're goin' fer to stay.
There 's grub to eat, an' grog for all,
   An' wages good to pay.
I 'll cross my legs upon a stool,
   An' never be a sailor;
I 'd rather be a butcher, or a
   Baker, or a tailor.

Roll, boys, roll, boys!
   Never mind the weather;
No matter how the wind blows,
   We 'll all get there together.

At the end of the song all the seamen stood up, joined hands, and
danced around, roaring out what Handsome called the "chor-i-us" in such
tremendous voices that the captain, who had come on deck, ran to the fore-

castle hatch to see what was going on. He dropped down among his men so suddenly that they all paused in silence, expecting an outbreak of anger. But the captain slowly realized the meaning of the scene upon which he had intruded, and said:

"All right, lads; amuse her and take good care of her. And when we get to New York I'll make it my business to find her father."

He was as good as his word, and in due time Molly was placed in the arms of her parents, who had been mourning her as dead. It was a joyous reunion, you may be sure. But all the rest of her life Molly remembered her strange Christmas eve at sea, and her wonderful Christmas-tree.

Santa Claus Street in Jingletown

BY SARAH J. BURKE

EVERY night when the lamps are lit,
And the stars through the curtain begin
    to peep —
When pussy has grown too tired to play,
    And has laid herself down on the rug to
    sleep —
When the spoon drops into the empty bowl
    (For baby has eaten her bread-and-milk),
And bright eyes hide behind drooping lids,
    Fringed with lashes as soft as silk —
When I lift my baby and fold her bib,
And carry her off to her little crib,
She whispers: "Before we cuddle down
Let us take a journey to Jingletown."

Oh, Jingletown is a wonderful town!
    Mother Goose lives on its finest square,
And little Jack Horner bought his pie
    At one of the bakers' shops there.
The House that Jack Built stands near the
    church

Where they sounded Cock Robin's knell,
And Little Bo-Peep there lost her sheep,
    When she took them to town to sell.
But the funniest thing of all is this —
You must stop at the toll-gate and pay a kiss!
For the tiniest tear or the slightest frown
Will keep a child out of Jingletown.

When we go, I follow my baby's lead,
    But, oh! she never wants to rest,
And I walk the streets of the queer old town
    In a never-ending quest.
But the street that my darling loves the most
    Is bordered with trees of evergreen,
Whose branches droop to the ground, and
    show
    The twinkling lights between.
There the merriest children swarm,
And my darling lingers, wrapped up warm
In her traveling-robe of eider-down —
Santa Claus Street, in Jingletown!

CHRISTMAS EVE

Christmas on the "Polly."

BY GRACE F. COOLIDGE

'T was the good ship *Polly*, and
   she sailed the wintry sea,
For ships must sail tho' fierce the gale,
   and a precious freight had she;
'T was the captain's little daughter stood
   beside her father's chair,
And illumed the dingy cabin with the sunshine of her hair.

With a yo-heave-ho, and a yo-heave-ho!
   For ships must sail
   Tho' fierce the gale
And loud the tempests blow.

And make believe the stove-pipe is a chimney—just for me?"

Loud laughed the jovial captain, and "By my
   faith," he cried,
"If he should come we 'll let him know he has
   a friend inside!"
And many a rugged sailor cast a loving glance
   that night

The captain's fingers rested on the pretty,
   curly head.
"To-morrow will be Christmas day," the
   little maiden said;
"Do you suppose that Santa Claus will find
   us on the sea,

At the stove-pipe where a lonely little
stocking fluttered white.

With a yo-heave-ho, and a yo-heave-ho!
For ships must sail
Tho' fierce the gale
And loud the tempests blow.

On the good ship *Polly* the Christmas
sun looked down,
And on a smiling little face beneath a
golden crown.
No happier child he saw that day, on
sea or on the land,
Than the captain's little daughter with
her treasures in her hand.

For never was a stocking so filled with curious
things!
There were bracelets made of pretty shells,
and rosy coral strings;
An elephant carved deftly from a bit of ivory
tusk;
A fan, an alligator's tooth, and a little bag of
musk.

Not a tar aboard the *Polly* but felt the
Christmas cheer,
For the captain's little daughter was to every
sailor dear.
They heard a Christmas carol in the shrieking
wintry gust,
For a little child had touched them by her
simple, loving trust.

With a yo-heave-ho, and a yo-heave-ho!
For ships must sail
Tho' fierce the gale
And loud the tempests blow.

CHRISTMAS IN THE MIDDLE AGES—BRINGING IN THE YULE LOG.

A GENTLE REMINDER

BY TUDOR JENKS

Time: Christmas morning.
Scene: Vicinity of everywhere. A cold day.

CHARACTERS.

A LITTLE GIRL, who is "not in it."
MR. SANTA CLAUS, a benevolent and well-meaning old gentleman, unusually fond of children.

COSTUMES.

LITTLE GIRL: à la ragbag.
MR. S. CLAUS: Furs and an engaging smile.

(MR. S. CLAUS enters during a paper snow-storm, carelessly swinging his empty pack.)

S. C.—My work is done, and now my goal
 Is a little north of the old north pole!

(LITTLE GIRL enters "left." Runs after S. C. and catches his coat.)

L.G.—But, Mr. Claus, one moment stay!
 Listen, before you hurry away;
 Neither in stocking nor on tree
 Has any present been left for me!

S. C.—You 've no present? That 's too bad!
 I 'd like to make all children glad.
 There 's something wrong; the fact is clear.
 I 'm very sorry indeed, my dear.

 I brought an endless lot of toys
 To millions and millions of girls and boys.
 But, still, there are so many about,
 Some have been overlooked, no doubt!

L. G.—Well, Santa Claus, I know you 're kind,
 And mean to bear us all in mind,
 But I can't see the reason why
 We poor are oftenest passed by.

S. C.—It 's true, my child. I can't but say
 I *have* a very curious way
 Of bringing presents to girls and boys
 Who have least need of pretty toys,
 And giving books, and dolls, and rings
 To those who already have such things.
 'T is done for a very curious reason,
 Suggested by the Christmas season:
 Should I make my gifts to those who need,
 'T would become a time of general greed,
 When all would think, "What shall we get?"
 "What shall we give?" they would quite forget.
 So when I send my gifts to-day
 'T is a hint: "You have plenty to give away."
 And then I leave some poor ones out
 That the richer may find, as they look about,
 Their opportunities near at hand
 In every corner of the land.
 My token to those who in plenty live
 Is a gentle reminder, meaning

Give!

(Curtain, and distribution of presents by the thoughtful audience after they reach home.)

"This is Sarah Jane Collins"

(*A Story Founded on Fact*)

BY JOHN J. Á BECKET

ROBABLY you never heard of Sarah Jane Collins. It would be surprising if you had. But I really feel that for the encouragement of small, unknown women, the world should hear of Sarah Jane, and of the way in which she conquered Santa Claus.

Sarah Jane Collins, at the time of this memorable achievement, was toppling to her ninth year. She was not heavily burdened with knowledge — not even when compared with other little nine-year-old girls. But she had learned one thing which stuck to her small mind like a bur. This was that Christmas is a time when Santa Claus simply rampages around shedding gifts upon children.

For some unaccountable reason, he had never shed any of his bounty on Sarah Jane.

She had expected, witnessed, and survived several Christmas days, not only without a single present, but without so much as a single card or note of regret from Santa Claus to atone for this absolute neglect. This might have shaken the faith of some small girls in the old Saint's being as generous as he is said to be. But it had not that effect on Sarah Jane.

However, she felt there was something wrong somewhere — or why did she not get Christmas presents? If he supposed that she did not care about them — why, then the Saint was sadly mistaken. Sarah Jane's soul was filled with a desire for Christmas presents.

This little girl lived in Barrytown with her mother and her brother John, who was eleven years old, but several years younger for his age than Sarah was. The chief industrial activity in Barrytown is coal-mining. John had an interest in a coal-mine. He was a "picker." As the coal comes streaming down the chute in the breaker the pickers snatch out the slate, as people do not like to buy coal and find large incombustible chunks of slate mingled with it. When John came home from picking, a stranger could not have told him from a black boy. He *was*, in fact, a very black boy; but I mean that any one would have imagined that he was a child of African descent. But you could n't expect John to sit handling lumps of coal all day in a place where the air is thick with flying coal-dust, and come out looking like a white boy.

The Collins family lived on the outskirts of the town, and beyond them were the coal-breakers, and heaps of "culm," and hills. In fact, the Collins mansion was on the crest of a hill. It was a wooden house two stories high; but it had a spare room, and that was rented to a Mr. Sullivan, who worked in the mine, of course, and who paid one dollar a week for his lodging.

Well, it was getting on toward Christmas. The river was frozen over, the culm-heaps wore white robes of snow, and the streets afforded splendid coasting. Sarah Jane, sliding wildly down the hill in a warm glow of delight, was really a much worthier subject for a sonnet than many that poets select. But in her small person lurked this memory of past Christmases, barren of gifts, and the remembrance was like a skeleton at the feast. When she and John made excursions through the business streets of the town, the shop-windows, stored with the things from which Santa Claus replenished his sleigh, brought home to Sarah still more strongly the past unfitness of things.

Although there was no selfishness or vanity in her nature, she never for a moment saw any reason why she should n't have presents. It was simply an oversight on Santa Claus' part. They lived so far out on the skirt of the town that the good Saint might be unaware that Sarah Jane Collins had waited there through several Christmas days — forgotten. It was only his unfortunate ignorance of her whereabouts that had led to her passing such fruitless Christmas days; that was all.

But Sarah Jane, with a most logical appreciation of the situation, argued that his ignorance had been quite enough to cause her to be overlooked in the past, and would doubtless prove sufficient this Christmas, unless she could bring herself to the good Saint's notice. So, about four days in advance of the eventful day, she presented herself before her mother and showed that worthy woman a small note.

"Mother," said Sarah Jane, "here's a letter which I 've written to Santa Claus. But I don't know how to get it to him."

"Sarah Jane! why have you written to Santa Claus?" exclaimed poor Mrs. Collins.

"So that he 'll know where I am and bring me my presents," said Sarah Jane, with the greatest gravity.

"Shall I read what you 've written to him?" asked her mother, with a troubled look.

"Yes."

Sarah Jane handed the sheet of white note-paper to her mother, who read, in large, laboriously formed letters, this communication of her daughter to Santa Claus:

December 21 92.

DEER SANTA CLAUS: I now take the plesure of riting to you to ask you if you would please remember me on Chrismas eve and my little brother becawse we are very poor and I have no papa to send any dollars but I will try and pay you bak when I grow a big woman and I am satisfyed with anything that you wish to bring me Deer Santa Claus. I have seen your stores and I think you have lots of pretty things in them and I would like to get something. We hold our Chrismas on monday Deer Santa Claus because we have sunday Scool on Chrismas day and our teacher says we must keep sunday so we don't have no scool for a whole week and so my mama says we can say our Chrismas day is on monday. Deer Santa Claus, Please remember the right howse, it is the howse nearest going up to the scool and ours is the only chimly on the whole block for my brother was out looking. This is the address, Deer Santa Claus.

SARAH JANE COLLINS
401 Blank Street.

Mrs. Collins held the letter in her hand and looked at her small daughter. The letter was addressed simply to "Mr. Santa Claus."

"Will I just drop it in the letter-box?" asked Sarah Jane, eagerly.

"I will attend to that for you, Sarah," said her mother. Mrs. Collins was somewhat distressed; but she had in her mind's eye some very kind people who, she thought, would know Santa Claus' address if she showed this letter to them.

So Sarah Jane intrusted the precious missive to the care of her mother. That good woman soon after put on her best shawl and bonnet, and went to a house where lived two young women whom she knew. They had very pretty faces and, what is better, very kind hearts. Mrs. Collins gave them the letter. They were much affected at Sarah Jane's direct appeal to Santa Claus, and when Mrs. Collins started on her way back it was with the comforting thought that Sarah Jane would not be left out this year.

She reported to the eager young correspondent that the letter had been sent on its way.

Then life took on new and rosy meanings for Sarah, and she almost counted the hours. Sarah frequently asked her mother if she thought Santa Claus could possibly miss the house. It would be trying if Sarah Jane's letter were to bring the old gentleman around their way, only to unload the gifts intended for her at a neighbor's house!

One day, as Mr. Sullivan was going to his room to remove the coal-dust which he had brought back with him from the mine, Sarah approached him in the small passageway and said :

"Mr. Sullivan, will you please clean out the chimney so when Santa Claus comes he can get down easily? I will mend and brush your clothes for a week if you will."

And Mr. Sullivan, who had a very large heart though he lived in such a small way, grinned and said, "Shure, I'll make it so clean that the ould Saint would just love to slide down it!" And if he did not clean the chimney with quite such scrupulous care as he might, it was because he knew Santa Claus was not a man to be balked in his gift-bearing course by a little soot in the chimney. Sarah religiously fulfilled her part of the contract, mending and brushing Mr. Sullivan's clothes every day with heroic fidelity.

Johnny Collins also was infected with the feverish delight with which Sarah Jane looked forward to the great day. She told her brother she had informed Santa Claus that they both wanted gifts. When Mrs. Collins saw her daughter casting glances at the clean chimney, she knew well what picture was in Sarah's mind.

On the evening of Sunday, Sarah went to her bed at her wonted hour for retiring, and tried to compose herself to sleep as quickly as usual. She feared that if Santa Claus were to come and find her awake he would take flight at once. Sarah Jane was convinced that the good old Saint could n't make a present while anybody looked on, because his generosity was of so modest a kind.

It was not easy to fall asleep, but at last Sarah was in the Land of Nod. When Mrs. Collins passed through the room, she saw the small girl with her hands folded outside the coverlet, and her eyes closed in slumber.

But she noticed that there was something on the headboard, and she stepped softly to the side of the bed to see what it was.

There, carefully pinned above the sleeping child, was a big sheet of light wrapping-paper, on which Sarah had neatly printed in large letters:

> THIS IS SARAH JANE COLLINS

She could hardly refrain from a laugh at the picture of her artless little girl sleeping so soundly with this label affixed above her, as if she were an exhibit in some fair. The bright notion of Sarah was clearly apparent:

Santa Claus should have no excuse for neglecting her *this* Christmas.   She had not left him a loophole for escape.   Those words told him clearly and unmistakably that "this was Sarah Jane Collins."   After her letter to him, this identification was the only thing necessary.

Sarah awoke at a very early hour, and sitting up in her bed, listened to hear if there was a sound of fairy-like sleigh-bells, or if there was a sliding noise in the chimney. She heard nothing. A glance at the bed showed her that it was not strewn with presents. She put back her hand to feel if the paper which she had prepared for the perfect enlightenment of Santa Claus was in its place; and then, thinking that she must give him every opportunity, she put her head back upon the pillow, and with great determination went to sleep again, and dreamed she was in a room full of presents, and that they were all for her and Johnny.

SARAH'S NOTICE TO SANTA CLAUS.

She got up at seven o'clock, and went all through the small house. There were no marks of Santa Claus. She scanned the opening of the chimney to see whether there were any indications of his having tried to get down there; but there was nothing anywhere to show that he had come near the house.

Her small countenance was very rueful, and after breakfast she and Johnny held a consultation. Could Santa Claus have gone astray? Or had he not received her letter? Sarah Jane felt like sitting down and having a good cry, if it *was* Christmas day. There were tears in her voice when she sought Mrs. Collins to see whether her mother could offer any reasonable excuse for this sad delay on Santa Claus' part.

" Why, my dear," said Mrs. Collins, cheerfully, "you told him that you had Monday as your Christmas day. This is only nine o'clock Monday morning, and so there is a great deal of time left for him to come in. But you and Johnny can go to the Sunday-school concert this afternoon — and don't fret ; I feel sure that he will come."

Mrs. Collins, in fact, knew from the kind young ladies who were so well acquainted with Santa Claus that he would surely come that afternoon. If there had been any doubt of it she would not have spoken so confidently to Sarah Jane. As it was, the little girl and Johnny went to the concert and enjoyed it very much.

They ran quickly home, however, and Sarah was in a tumult of agitated hopes when she burst into the house. And the front-room door was just a little ajar, as if some visitor had not quite closed it after him. Sarah Jane pushed the door wide open, and flew into the room with a cry of delight.

There in the corner stood the most beautiful little Christmas-tree!

The wax tapers on it were shining like stars, and festoons of white pop-corn were wreathed from bough to bough, as if the tree had traveled through a snow-storm. Then the presents! There were things in bright-colored paper tied with pretty ribbons in a way so dainty and coquettish that it was surprising an old man like Santa Claus could have done it.

Oh, how full and beautiful that Christmas-tree looked to Sarah Jane, who danced with delight before it, her eyes shining, and her whole face one broad, happy smile! Then, although it was hard to leave the lively spectacle even for a moment, she ran up to her mother, who was seated quietly in the other room, and shouted:

" Oh, mama, he 's been here. Did n't you hear him ? Come in and see the tree!"

She grasped her mother's hand and hurried her into the next room. And after they had looked at the brilliant tree, and enjoyed it thoroughly, Sarah Jane had to go and get Mr. Sullivan, that he, too, might enjoy the beautiful sight.

" It 's mine," said Sarah Jane to him, rather grandly, standing as tall as she could — "mine and Johnny's. I wrote Santa Claus a letter for it."

" Shure, he 's a foine, daycent ould man !" said Mr. Sullivan, with great consideration.

"But he did n't come down the chimney," said Sarah Jane, animatedly. "Don't you see that tree is too big for the chimney?"

"And afther my cl'aning it so foine, and you a-mendin' me clothes fur a whole week!" cried Mr. Sullivan.

"Oh, that 's all right!" returned Sarah Jane, heartily.

"He came in at the door with it," said Johnny. "The boys at the mine told me he could open any door he wanted to."

But no matter how he came — he had come. And there was the proof of it — that gay, luminous tree. And the presents were so exactly what Sarah wanted that she exclaimed to her mother, "He *must* have known me. But was n't it lucky I sent him that letter?"

The Christmas-Tree Lights

BY ANNIE WILLIS McCULLOUGH

WHEN holiday week 's almost over,
  And broken are some of the toys,
When Christmas-tree needles are dropping,
  And drums will not give out a noise,

When some one has said, "It 's a nuisance;
  This tree *must* be carried away,"
And we stand around and look gloomy,
  And beg for it "just one more day,"

There 's one thing that keeps up our spirits:
  The best of the week's merry nights
Is just at the last, when we children
  May blow out the Christmas-tree lights.

The little tots, Doris and Douglas,
  They blow out the ones lowest down.
Their faces get redder and redder;
  Their foreheads are all in a frown.

Then Alice, the next high by measure,
  Puts out all the candles half low;
And then I, the eldest and tallest,
  I blow, and I *blow*, and I ʙʟᴏᴡ!

But even *I* can't reach the top ones,
  So father lifts up Baby Grace;
Her dear little mouth is a circle,
  All wrinkled her sweet little face.

She blows out the tiptopmost candles;
  We clap and hurrah when she 's done;
And that is the end of the Christmas,
  The very — last — bit — of — the — fun!

   *   *   *   *   *

But all through the year it 's a pleasure
  To think of our holiday nights —
The best coming last, when we children
  May blow out the Christmas-tree lights.

St. Nicholas will soon be here
He brings you love, he brings
A merrie Christmas,
A glad New Year.

E·R·S

A CHRISTMAS GOBLIN

BY SUSAN HARTLEY SWETT

The calm moon smiled — he looked
  so weird;
The old pine wagged its frosty beard.

THERE was a funny goblin
  Who lived in the wood lane.
He goggles wore, and, though three-score,
  Quite bald and sadly plain,
And not as nimble in his mind
As many a goblin one might find.

Much pleased with his own person
  And his own wit was he;
And so he said, with lofty head:
  " It would not Christmas be
Without *me* in the town to-night
To make the merry hours more bright!

" And though at home they 'll miss me,
  Unto the Squire's I 'll speed,
To fill folk's dreams with magic gleams,
  And in the dance to lead.
My presence always lends a grace
To holidays, in any place."

He rode a lop-eared rabbit;
  He wore a coat of red;
His peaked hat this way and that
  Bobbed when he moved his head.

He reached the Squire's at midnight,
  And gaily entered in.
Before the fire a cricket choir
  Sang to the violin;
But when they saw the goblin, they
All dropped their bows and swooned
  away!

Jack Frost, who stood there sketching
  Upon the window-pane
Some pictures white for day's delight,
  Became as limp as rain;
And all his drawings looked like O's,
Or like the goblin's funny nose!

While Santa Claus, who entered
  Just then the chimney way,
Spilled half his pack, and cried, " Alack ! "
  And three small mice in gray,
Who danced a measure on the floor,
Fled, squeaking, by a private door!

The maid woke screaming from her sleep —
  Such frightful dreams had she;
The watch-dogs howled, the poodle growled,
  The parrot croaked " Dear me ! "

The elves all up the chimney fled;
A spider, spinning. dropped her thread!

The noise awoke Grimalkin,
  So wise and fierce and black,
Who, with a cry both loud and high,
  Sprang at the goblin's back!
Home for his life the goblin flew;
Puss following — the watch-dog, too.

" I did my duty nobly,"
  Next morn the goblin said.
" I made a great sensation,
  And every rival fled!
You should have heard the wild applause!
Why, no one thought of Santa Claus!"

Then an old crow, who calmly
  Was practising a caw
To aid the Christmas music,
  Blinked twice, and said, " Haw-haw!

"HOME FOR HIS LIFE THE GOBLIN FLEW."

The more conceited people grow,
The less they please — the less they know!"

"HE RODE A LOP-EARED RABBIT."

London Christmas Pantomimes

BY ELIZABETH ROBINS PENNELL

OU might as well try to imagine a Christmas at home without presents as a Christmas in London without pantomimes. The best of it is that the pantomimes do not, like too many candies or toys, come to an end with Christmas week. They have a delightful way of making the Christmas holidays last until the first spring flowers are out in the woods and fields, and the first Easter eggs in the shop windows. If you cannot go to see them before the 1st of January, you need not be troubled as you would if Christmas presents had not come long before New Year's day. There will be plenty of chances next month, and the month after, and even the month after that.

It is best to explain in the very beginning that they are not pantomimes at all. Englishmen love to call things by the names they have long outgrown, and because once there were really pantomimes in which not a word was spoken, these Christmas entertainments of nowadays, in which there is plenty of talking and even singing, must keep the old name.

And if they are not pantomimes, what are they then, do you ask? It is much easier to say what they are not. Shows so wonderful and gorgeous you might well think were never to be seen this side of fairyland. They are full of dancing and marching, of joking and tumbling, of gay music and still gayer lights. They take you into all sorts of strange places and introduce you to old friends you have loved ever since you can remember: to Ali Baba and the Forty Thieves, to Aladdin and the wonderful lamp, to Bluebeard and Fatima, to Robinson Crusoe and Friday. To be sure, you would never recognize them if their names were not given in the program, but nevertheless they are as ready to amuse you on the stage as they ever were in the story-book. Besides, you learn a great deal about them you never knew before. And then, too, there are beasts or birds or fish straight from Wonderland; and just as you begin to feel that you have seen sights enough for one day, hey, presto! the scene changes and in come Columbine

and Harlequin, clown and Pantaloon, policemen and bad boys, shopkeepers
and market-women.

If you lived in London it would not be worth while for me to tell you
that the greatest pantomime of all is to be seen at Drury Lane. Every
London child, from the Queen's grandson to the little street Arab, knows
Drury Lane Theater as well as, if not better than, Westminster Abbey or
St. Paul's. For three, sometimes four, months it belongs to him in a way;
for, though grown-up people go to see the pantomime, every one knows it
is meant specially for the children.

You would not doubt this for a moment had you been with me one
Saturday afternoon, when I went to Drury Lane. I thought I had come in
good time, but once I was inside the door I heard the loudest, merriest singing, so that a short delay at the ticket-office made me quite impatient.

When I was shown to my seat, to my surprise the curtain was still down.
The music, however, had begun, and, looking around, I saw that the great
theater was packed from top to bottom with children, and all were singing
an accompaniment to the orchestra. Box above box, balcony above balcony, was lined with little faces: mothers and fathers, older brothers and
sisters, thoughtfully taking back seats, while I don't know how many schools
had emptied their children into the pit. You must know that the part of the
theater called the parquet with us is in England the pit, only a few of the
front rows being reserved.

"God save the Queen!" struck up the band. "Long may she reign
over us!" sang the children. It would have put you into a good humor at
once merely to look up and down and all around at the beaming faces and
open mouths.

Bang, bang! went the bass drum, the singing stopped, up went the curtain, and we beheld an earthly paradise where huge lilac-trees made a pretty
bower for dancing girls, who, as their loose trousers and clinging skirts
showed, had just stepped out of the "Arabian Nights." In the midst of their
dancing, a hansom, the first, I am sure, that was ever seen in the Moham-
medan paradise, drove up, and Aladdin jumped out. He had come with a
message from Mr. Augustus Harris, the manager of Drury Lane, who
wanted a new Eastern story. Aladdin, you must know, was the hero of the
pantomimes the year before; that he remained with Mr. Harris as his
messenger is not to be wondered at, since on the Drury Lane stage as
strange things happen as in Scheherazade's stories. What could be stranger,
for instance, than that forty young Arabian knights should consent to leave
paradise and humming-birds' eggs and jasmine wine to become forty thieves!
And yet, so willing were they that when Aladdin suggested it they danced

"BOX ABOVE BOX, BALCONY ABOVE BALCONY, WAS
LINED WITH LITTLE FACES."

and sang with joy at the very thought of the change. So I found out something the story does not tell me—where the Forty Thieves came from!

This being pleasantly settled, the next thing was to find Ali Baba, for without him there would have been no story to tell of the thieves. In a moment, houris and knights, Aladdin and lilacs, had disappeared, and we were in the bazaar of an Eastern city, with people going and coming. On one side was Ali Baba's shop; on the other, Cassim's. "No connection with the shop opposite!" was posted up on each. You remember, of course, how little friendship there was between the brothers. When Morgiana and Ganem, Ali Baba and Cogia, Cassim Baba and his wife, met in front of the shops—"Well, I was astonished!" as Joey the clown said afterward in the harlequinade. Ali Baba was very much shabbier and more disreputable than I expected; Cogia, it was quite plain, was just making believe to be a woman; Morgiana's silks and sashes were not in the least like the clothes I supposed slaves usually wore. And I could only put down to Oriental manners the fact that every few minutes, no matter what they were talking about, they were sure to sing and dance. This was a fine opportunity for the children who were looking on.

"You 're all very fine and large, because you 've heaps of cash,"

sang Cogia to the wealthy sister and brother. And then all the children came in with the chorus,

"You 're all very fine and large,"

as if they had lived in the same street with Ali and Cassim all their lives, and the leader of the orchestra turned round and kept time for them. It was great fun.

When they were all singing together it seemed as if the Babas must have forgotten the family quarrels. But not a bit of it. "I 've an idea," whispered Cassim to his wife:

"The donkey that we 've bought
Has proved more vicious than at first we thought.
He 's almost sure to kill some one or other,
So I propose to give him to my brother!"

MR. AND MRS. ALI BABA.

Ganem brought in the donkey. And what was the first thing it did? It knocked over Cassim with its flying heels; it stood on its head in the corner; it gave Cogia a friendly embrace; it danced, it turned somersaults, and at last stretched itself full length on Cassim's counter. If such a donkey were in the Zoo, the bear-pit and the monkey-house would be deserted.

And now you know what is going to happen. Bazaar and Baba family disappear in their turn, and here we are away in the depths of the forest. Dozens of little monkeys are running and playing and leaping, while two or three swing backward and forward on long ropes all of flowers hanging from the very tallest of trees. Ali Baba and Ganem with hatchets and caskets come to get wood, the faithful donkey just at their heels, and the monkeys vanish; while Cogia and Morgiana bring their luncheon, lobster and tongue, pies and sauces, for all the world as if they were picnicking in an English instead of an "Arabian Nights" forest. A large monkey joins the family circle, and then what a frolic he and the donkey have! They steal the luncheon, put their feet in the basket, upset the pepper and set poor Ali Baba to sneezing; they dance and play leap-frog, they fight and "make up again"; the monkey sits on the donkey, the donkey puts his head on the monkey's knees. "But what 's that?" cries Ganem. "What 's what?"

echoes Ali Baba. There is a sound of trumpets in the distance. It comes nearer and nearer.

"The famous Forty Thieves, I should n't wonder!" Ali declares, and away they all run to hide, monkey and donkey jumping together into a barrel; and the next minute, to the loudest music,—for these are gay robbers and defy the police,—the Forty Thieves march out from under the trees. They are dressed in a style befitting gentlemen late from an Eastern paradise and now engaged in parading through forests at noon with bags of precious stones over their shoulders. The captain, resplendent in gold-embroidered cloak and waving plumes, leads the way; at his side the Honorary Secretary, Ally Sloper, a hideous creature with bald head and monstrous nose, who got into paradise by mistake, but into his present position by his own free will.

THE HONORARY SECRETARY, ALLY SLOPER.

"Open sesame!" shouts the captain.

With a deep booming and banging, the rock at one side opens, and then emeralds and diamonds and rubies are stored.

"Shut sesame!" commands the captain.

Another great booming and banging, and soon, singing gaily, the thieves are off to their club.

And now it is Ali Baba's turn to open and shut sesame, and the treasures that have just been brought to the cave are soon on their way out of the forest, this time on the donkey's back. It is very much more real when you see it all than when you just read about it.

There would be no use for railroads in Drury Lane country. The treasure-finders are scarcely out of sight of the cave when, lo and behold! here they are in Ali Baba's humble home. You know already what a blunder it was to borrow the measure from Cassim's wife. She finds, busybody that she is, the telltale piece of gold sticking to the lard she has put at the bottom. Of course no one can tell where it came from, but just then what should those two troublesome beasts do but dip hoofs and paws into the money-bag and jingle it up and down! There is no help for it. The secret must be shared with Cassim or else he will call the police. But, in the meantime, in comes a man to be shaved, for Ali Baba is a barber by profession. The monkey watches, and no sooner is he left alone in the shop with the donkey than he puts the latter in the chair and himself seizes the razor.

The white lather comes out of the basin in great stiff patches and foamy flakes. The donkey's eyes, ears, mouth are soon covered, and he never moves. But with the first stroke of the razor, the chair is kicked over, and he is in a corner spluttering and shaking his head angrily. In a moment he catches sight of the monkey grinning at him in derision. And now there is a very interesting fight, I promise you. The looking-glass crashes over the donkey's head, the table breaks into splinters under the monkey's weight. It is a good thing for Ali Baba that he has just come into a fortune, for there will be bills to pay. The monkey tries to escape, but where shall he go? Quick as thought he springs up to the opera-box close to the stage, and off he runs on the very edge of boxes and balcony. Little lookers-on jump back with frightened faces. But the donkey is after the fugitive and soon overtakes him. Down he slips, holding on by his hands, his feet dangling over the heads of the people in the pit. Then both sit and rest, the monkey seizing a program from the nearest child to fan itself. And then, I hardly know how it happens, they are running a race, one on one side of the house, one on the other. Who will win? Neither. They jump down from the opposite boxes at the same moment, meet

THE DONKEY AND THE MONKEY MAKE A VISIT.

in the middle of the stage, embrace, make a great ball of themselves, and roll over and over, off the stage. I don't think I should care to live in Ali Baba's "humble home" with two such pets about.

Have you not always wished to see the inside of that famous cave? Now

that we see it, I do not think it is disappointing.   Great walls and lofty
ceiling of brown rock are lighted by huge brass lamps; mysterious narrow
passages glitter with gold and lead to untold treasures.   I for my part am
not surprised that Cassim will not go, despite the efforts of Ali Baba and
Cogia.

Boom, boom! bang, bang! and not only the door at the mouth of the
cave high above his head, but all those opening into the glittering passages
are shut.   It is too late.   In vain does he shout, "Open sausages!   Open
sardines!"   In vain does he weep and wail.   But some one outside gives
the true password, and bang, boom! boom, bang! the doors are open
again.

Yet even now there is no escape.   In march, not forty, but four hundred
and more thieves, all in silks and satins, in velvet and plush of every color,
with gold and silver armor and jeweled spears and swords.   There is no
doubt of the industry of these gentlemen robbers.   They carry the proof on
their backs.   Forward comes the captain, outshining all in the glory of his
black-and-silver brocade, his jewels sparkling from arms and neck and
waist, and his cloak so long that it must be borne by a dozen tiny pages.
Above, at the entrance of the cave, stands Ally Sloper, his vermilion cloak
held out by his arms so that he looks like a great red bat.

So gay are the thieves that their meeting is always the signal for song.
But I don't think any one pays much attention to the singing.   I suppose
the upshot of their visit to the cave is the death of Cassim, for not long after
he is brought home, in four pieces, by Ali Baba and Cogia.   Everything
now happens very much as it does in the story-book, only the Baba family
are more cheerful in their mourning than you might have expected.   Ali's
and Cogia's new clothes are in worse taste than even their previous inex-
perience would warrant; while Cogia, now that she has no work to do,
brings home all the stray children she finds in the street.

She is not pretty to look at, in her fine new blue-spangled trousers,
short yellow-spangled skirts, and red-spangled bodice, two long pigtails
dangling down her back, a little blue fan in her hand.   But, to make up for
it, nothing could be prettier than the screaming, laughing children who
gather around her.   I fancy it is because they are little Eastern children
that they wear such queer long sage-green gowns, with broad belts and
jaunty caps.

Now they must go to bed, says their adopted mother.   Will they be
good children?   "Yes, indeed! as good as good can be."   But once her
back is turned, the fun begins.   Off come gowns and belts, blue petticoats
and caps, and there they are in long white night-gowns and tasseled night-

caps. In another minute they are sitting on the floor pulling off their shoes, and all the time they are singing, and, whenever they have the opportunity, dancing in time to the music.

Clothes are carefully folded; each seizes her pile, too big for some tiny arms, and a shoe drops here, a cap there; but the little ones dance bravely in and out—not to bed, however, for here they are again, now armed with

"THERE THEY STAND IN TWO ROWS, GREAT TALL JARS WITH HEADS PEEPING OUT OF THEM."

pillows. Our pillow-fights at school, as I remember them, were very rough and ugly compared with this fairy game, in which white figures dance to and fro, and white pillows wave up and down as yellow curly heads and dangling tassels dodge them.

How the children in pit and boxes applaud! While they are still clapping, the children on the stage run out and bring back a lady in black, and there is more applause, for she it is who has taught them to go singing and dancing to bed. Whenever the children are applauded at Drury Lane, and you may be sure they always are, they bring forward their dancing-mistress, as if to remind you that to her must be given all the praise for what they do.

While they have been pillow-fighting, Abdallah, the captain of the thieves, has placed his jars in Ali Baba's court. There they stand in two rows, great tall jars with heads peeping out of them. The plot is laid. Ali Baba and his household must be slain this night. But Morgiana by

ALICE HAD FALLEN ASLEEP UNDER A LARGE TREE.

herself is a fair match for Abdallah with all his followers. To tell the truth, I always thought the thieves in the story sad cowards to let themselves be scalded to death by one slave-girl without a struggle; and now that I have looked on at their last moments, I have a still poorer opinion of them. For forty young robbers, boldly defiant in the daytime, well armed and wide awake too,—for they had their heads out of the jar but a minute before,— to be thus cowed by a girl with a tiny watering-pot and a boy with a dagger quite as tiny! Well, it is shameful, and I am not in the least sorry for them.

Abdallah, nothing daunted, comes back to Ali Baba with some story about his jars. Morgiana is called upon to dance, and she does so, to the captain's sorrow. He leans forward to applaud; in goes the dagger; he falls in Cogia's arms. Now, no story is a story unless in the end every one marries and lives happy ever afterward. Mrs. Cassim, the widow, marries that ugly thief Ally Sloper — the sly one, he knew better than to put himself like oil into a jar! Morgiana and Ganem join hands. And immediately the captain (no doctors needed here!) comes to life without any difficulty. His services will be in demand to-morrow night, he fears, and so he really could not remain dead. Now, I protest that 's all wrong. The next thing we know, Cinderella won't marry the prince, Jack won't kill the giant, Robinson Crusoe won't find his man Friday. But it 's no use protesting. Ali Baba and, what is more, Morgiana, is satisfied; and with their victim and Ally Sloper and the donkey and Ganem, and Cogia and Mrs. Cassim, they sing and dance good-by to us.

Do you think this is the end? Far from it; we're only at the beginning, you might say. It's a good deal to see in one afternoon, I must admit, and I notice that the children before me and on every side of me no longer join in the chorus.

Soon after Ali Baba and his friends have disappeared, we find ourselves in the Temple of Fame — a huge statue of Queen Victoria in the center, women in silken robes and men in glittering armor surrounding it. Red, green, golden lights burn from every side. Whatever it may mean, I am quite sure this meeting in the Temple of Fame is well worth looking at.

And now surely this is the end? Not yet; patience a minute. From the Temple of Fame we are carried to a London street, where we find those best of all old friends, Columbine, twirling and pirouetting, Harlequin waving his magic wand. The clown plays his tricks, turns his somersaults, poor Pantaloon is fooled; the policeman gets the worst of it; the bad boys escape. It is the same old story you know so well, but which somehow always makes you laugh as if it were brand-new.

But the best fun of all is when Joey, having dressed a little squealing black pig in baby-clothes, puts it in the baby-carriage, and the pig gets loose

THE CHESHIRE CAT AND THE WHITE RABBIT.   ALICE AND THE DORMOUSE.

and jumps from the stage down upon the big drum. The drummer does not like it; but the children do, and, amid shouts of laughter, the pig is caught and handed to the clown and wheeled out in the carriage. Then Joey gets rid of the policeman for a moment, and brings from the nearest shop a small

"TWINKLE, TWINKLE, LITTLE BAT!"

barrel, from which he takes handfuls of toy crackers and flings them to the nearest children in the audience. A little girl in white is perched up on the front seat of a box. "There 's my little sweetheart!" he cries in his cracked voice, and throws her one. In the box above a boy leans far over with hand outstretched. The clown holds up a cracker, but just as the little fingers are about to close on it, he pulls it away. He must always have his joke, you see. What a laugh there is on every side! But the next minute half a dozen pretty, gay-colored crackers are thrown into the same box. No matter what changes there may be each new year at Drury Lane, the clown never forgets his barrel of crackers.

Now I hope you have some idea of what London Christmas pantomimes are like. There are three or four theaters besides Drury Lane where you can go to see them. A different story is presented in each, but whether the hero is Ali Baba or Aladdin, Bluebeard or Robinson Crusoe, you always may be sure there will be dancing and singing, gay dresses, and crowds of men and women to wear them.

Last year, however, there was one Christmas entertainment not in the least like the others, but which I thought the best of all. It was a performance of "Alice in Wonderland," at the Prince of Wales Theater. It seemed too good to be true, to have the opportunity of beholding Alice and the extraordinary and delightful "creatures" which she met in her two famous journeys. A few of these creatures, the Lizard, the Mouse, and the Puppy, for example, were missing; and on the stage Alice did not meet with some adventures recorded in the book. Her head did not go wandering among the topmost branches of trees to be mistaken for a serpent, neither did she shrink until her chin and feet met with a violent blow. But most of the entertaining dwellers in Wonderland and Looking-Glass Country—the Rabbit and the Caterpillar, the Mad Hatter, the March Hare, the Dormouse, the Cards and Chessmen and their Kings and Queens, Tweedledum and Twee-dledee, Humpty-Dumpty, and the Knights — were there ; and as for adven tures, if several were left out, there were still many presented — enough for one afternoon.

Alice was, just as you would suppose, a pretty little girl in a simple white frock, and with long hair hanging down her back. She had fallen asleep, it seemed, under a large tree with wide-spreading branches, and when the cur tain went up we saw the kind fairies — they were not any older than Alice — who brought her strange dreams. It is pleasant traveling in Wonderland. Alice had scarcely started when she met the White Rabbit "splendidly dressed" in a jaunty jacket, as you see him in the picture, and in woolly rabbit-skin trousers, a high collar and bright-red necktie. In his waistcoat-pocket he wore his watch, like any other gentleman. He was a very timid rabbit, and the first word sent him scurrying away. The green Caterpillar sat smoking its hooka on the mushroom, and made Alice recite, "You are old, Father William," while the foliage in the background opened, and there we

THE TEA-PARTY.

From a photograph by Elliott and Fry, London

saw the old man turning his somersaults, standing on his head, balancing the eel on his nose, kicking his son down-stairs. The Duchess, who was much better-looking than her pictures, though ugly enough, came in with the baby ; the Cook, neat and pretty, her sleeves rolled up, a fresh white cap on her curly hair, followed with her pepper-pot, and the Cheshire Cat, with his grin. The latter was as accomplished as the donkey at Drury Lane, and sang and danced with Alice, grinning all the time.

I take it for granted you have read the two books about Alice. Indeed, I believe there are few young people who can read English who do not know them both by heart. You remember, then, the tea-party? Of all her adventures, it was always my favorite, and I could have clapped my hands with the children when I saw the Mad Hatter and the March Hare bring in the table with the tea-things on it. Among the cups and saucers and bread-and-butter was a soft, gray something, curled up like a pussy-cat. The Mad Hatter picked it up and put it on a chair between himself and the March Hare. It was the Dormouse — the tiniest, sweetest, sleepiest Dormouse you can imagine. Its little gray head was down on the table at once, and it was having its own dreams. The March Hare wore a staring red waistcoat, and around his left ear was a wreath of roses. He looked very mad. So did the Hatter, in blue-and-white plaid trousers and an enormous gray hat

From a photograph by Elliott and Fry, London.
ALICE, THE MOCK TURTLE, AND THE GRYPHON.

placarded with its price. As you know, it was always tea-time with them, and, drinking and eating, they began at once their talk — mad as themselves. Every now and then the Dormouse woke up for a minute, to join in with the prettiest little voice. I wish you could have heard the story of Elsie, Lacie, and Tillie, who lived at the bottom of a well on treacle, and the solemn way in which, when Alice said they must have been ill, it answered:

"So they were! very ill!"

But what a sleepy Dormouse! Down went the little gray head after every few words, and the March Hare had to push and push it to keep it awake till the end of the story. But then it was such a very young Dormouse — not more than six years old certainly.

When the Mad Hatter and the March Hare had carried out the table and the sleeping Dormouse, I was sorry to see they did not play croquet with flamingoes and hedgehogs. However, the Mock Turtle and the Gryphon danced the Lobster Quadrille, and that is a sight only to be seen in dreams, I can assure you. The two "creatures" looked exactly as they do in the pictures in Mr. Carroll's book. When little Alice stood between the tall green Gryphon, whose brilliant wings flapped with every movement, and the awkward Mock Turtle, whose long tail dragged on the floor, I thought of Beauty and the Beast; only here were two Beasts to one Beauty.

It would be simply impossible to describe all the things I dreamed with Alice that afternoon. For her dream did not end with the trial of the Knave of Hearts, who stole those tarts and took them quite away, nor when the little Dormouse slept in the very face of the court, and the White Rabbit, as Herald, blew many blasts on his trumpet, and the Mad Hatter, tea-cup in hand, gave his evidence, and Alice herself pronounced the verdict —" Not guilty."

Without once waking up, she went straight from Wonderland into Looking-Glass Country, where white and red Chessmen sang and danced, Humpty-Dumpty sat on the wall and had his great fall, and Tweedledum

From a photograph by Elliott and Fry, London.
TWEEDLEDUM AND TWEEDLEDEE.

and Tweedledee fought their great battle. If only you could have seen Tweedledum and Tweedledee—fat, over grown boys with tiny caps on their heads—when they and Alice played " Here we go round the mulberry-bush "! Why, such great fun they seemed to be having that it made, one feel like jumping up, joining hands, and going round the mulberry-bush with them. And the way Tweedledum cried over his rattle! I know a little girl who, when she is angry, screams so loud her father calls her "the

Tuscaroarer"; but her screams could not compare with Tweedledum's.
And then the battle! To see those two big boys, who ought to have
known better, tying blankets and bolsters around their waists, and sticking
coal-scuttles on their heads—well, if it had not all happened in a dream,
certainly it would have shocked a careful housewife.

After the Carpenter and the Walrus had eaten up the oysters, and the
Lion and the Unicorn had fought for the crown, Alice was made Queen,
and gave her party, to which all the Chessmen came. The Cook brought
in the Leg of Mutton on a big dish, and up it jumped and made a bow; the

Chess-men

Plum-Pudding walked in, and when Alice cut out a great slice, a little wee
voice, very like that of the Dormouse, cried from the inside:

"I wonder how you would like it if I were to cut a slice out of you!"

Almost at once the banquet-hall, the new Queen, and all her guests disappeared, and Alice was again sleeping in the big chair under the tree. Once
more the fairies waved their wands, and this time Alice rubbed her eyes.

"Oh, I've had such a curious dream!" she said when she awoke.
"And a pleasant dream, too," I think all those who woke up with her said
to themselves.

Just let me say a few more words, to tell you that one of the charms of
the performance was the pleasure of the children who took part in it—and
all but two of the performers were children. You forgot that they were not

playing merely to amuse themselves. That they were working seemed as unlikely as that birds are practising their scales when they sing.

Alice's dream ended in due time; but that is no reason why she may not dream again. The pantomimes of last winter came to an end; but this season new ones will take their place, and may you and I be in London to see!

"HUMPTY-DUMPTY SAT ON A WALL."

If You 're Good

BY JAMES COURTNEY CHALLISS

SANTA CLAUS 'll come to-night,
    If you 're *good*.
And do what you know is right,
    As you should;
Down the chimney he will creep,
Bringing you a woolly sheep,
And a doll that goes to sleep —
    If you 're *good*.

Santa Claus will drive his sleigh
    Through the wood,
But he 'll come around this way,
    If you 're good,
With a wind-up bird that sings,
And a puzzle made of rings, —
Jumping-jacks and funny things, —
    If you 're *good*.

He will bring you cars that "go,"
    If you 're good,
And a rocking-horsey — *oh !*
    If he would!
And a dolly, if you please,
That says "Mama!" when you squeeze
It — he 'll bring you one of these,
    If you 're *good*.

Santa grieves when you are bad,
    As he should;
But it makes him very glad
    When you 're good.
He is wise, and he 's a dear;
Just do right and never fear;
He 'll remember you each year,
    If you 're *good*.

Santa Claus and the Mouse

BY EMILIE POULSSON

ONE Christmas eve, when Santa
  Claus
Came to a certain house
To fill the children's stockings
  there,
He found a little mouse.

"A merry Christmas, little friend,"
Said Santa, good and kind.
"The same to you, sir," said the
  mouse;
"I thought you would n't mind

"If I should stay awake to-night
And watch you for a while."
"You 're very welcome, little
  mouse,"
Said Santa, with a smile.

And then he filled the stockings
  up
Before the mouse could wink—
From toe to top, from top to toe,
There was n't left a chink.

"Now, they won't hold another thing,"
Said Santa Claus, with pride.
A twinkle came in mouse's eyes,
But humbly he replied:

"It 's not polite to contradict,—
Your pardon I implore,—
But in the fullest stocking there
I could put one thing more."

"Oh, ho!" laughed Santa, "silly
  mouse!
Don't I know how to pack?
By filling stockings all these
  years,
I should have learned the
  knack."

And then he took the stocking
  down
From where it hung so high,
And said: "Now put in one thing
  more;
I give you leave to try."

The mousie chuckled to himself,
And then he softly stole
Right to the stocking's crowded
  toe
And gnawed a little hole!

"Now, if you please, good Santa
  Claus,
I 've put in one thing more;
For you will own that little
  hole
Was not in there before."

How Santa Claus did laugh and
  laugh!
And then he gaily spoke:
"Well! you shall have a Christmas
  cheese
For that nice little joke."

MR. SNOWBIRD SPENDS CHRISTMAS DAY WITH BR'ER RABBIT.

·THE·BEST·TREE·

By Janet Henderson.

KARL lay on the floor by the
    firelight bright
    Thinking about the trees.
"I love them all," he said to himself,
    As he named them over with ease;
"The chestnut, ash, and oak so high,
    The pine with its needle leaves,
The spruce, and cedar, and hemlock green,
    And the maple with its keys.

"The dainty willow with pussies gray,
    The birch with bark so white,
The apple-tree with its blossoms sweet,
    And the fruit so red and bright.
But the one I love the *best* of all
    Blooms and bears fruit
      together;
It is sure to be filled at
    this time of the
    year,
    Whatever may be
      the weather.

"Its blossoms are blue
    and yellow and red,
    All shining with silvery hue.
There are stems of golden and sil-
    ver thread,
    And candles that glisten like dew.
With such wonderful fruit there 's none can compare;
    From lowest to topmost bough
Every sort of a toy is swinging in air —
    Jumping frogs, and cats that 'me-ow.'

"There are trumpets, and balls, and dolls
    that talk,
  And drums, and whistles that blow,
And guns, and whips, and horses that walk,
  And books; and wagons that go.
There are musical tops, and boats that sail,
  And puzzles, and knives, and games;
There are Noah's arks, and also a whale,
  And boxes, and ribbons, and reins.

"There's candy and oranges, skates and sleds,
  And mugs for good little girls,
And cradles, and clothes for dollies' beds,
  And dolls with hair in curls.

There are fans for girls and tools for
    boys,
  And handkerchiefs, rattles, and ties,
And horns, and bells, and such-like toys,
  And tea-sets and candy pies.

"Oh! what a sight is this wonderful tree,
  With its gifts that sparkle and hide!
Other trees may be good, but there's none
    for me
Like the beautiful merry Christmas-tree
  With its branches spreading wide,—
The merry, beautiful, sparkling tree
  That blossoms at Christmas-tide."

COUSIN JANE'S MISTAKE

BY MARY E. BRADLEY

COUSIN JANE was an elderly lady who had never married, and who had outlived all her near relatives. A few cousins, some young and some old, some poor and some well-to-do, were all her kinsfolk; and having more money than she chose to spend for herself, she was generous to these cousins on birthdays and holidays.

One Christmas-time she was putting up a number of parcels to be sent by express to a number of people. Through an interruption, which caused some confusion in her arrangements and some hurry in their completion, two of the packages were misdirected; the one intended for a certain Miss Martha Redfield being carefully addressed to Miss Mary Rutherford, while Mary's parcel was as plainly marked with Martha's name. In her haste, and in the darkness of the waning afternoon, Cousin Jane had also, quite unconsciously, exchanged her presentation cards, so that the message meant for Martha went into the box meant for Mary, and *vice versa*.

In due time each parcel was delivered according to its direction, if not according to intention; and when Martha Redfield, a bright-eyed girl of fifteen, opened hers, she beheld a charming box decorated with painted flowers and bows of satin ribbon.

" A box of candy! " she exclaimed in a tone of surprise.

" Is that all?" asked her mother, in a tone of disappointment. "Well, dear," she added more cheerfully, " you don't often have a present of candy. It will be a treat for you."

" Of course it will," said Martha.

Still, in each face was a wondering and unsatisfied expression.

" I don't know what I expected," Martha remarked presently, with a half-laugh. "And you know, mother, that Cousin Jane is so good to us that, of course, I ought to be pleased with *anything* she sends. But — somehow —"

"It seems as if, when she was spending so much as this thing must have cost," added Mrs. Redfield, "she might better have sent you something useful."

"Well, I don't know."

Martha turned about, with a sudden change of tone:

"I 'm not sure but I like this better, after all. Cousin Jane always has sent useful things, because she knew we needed them. But just for once to be treated as if she *did n't* know we needed them!—as if we had as good a right to eat real good candy as her *rich* cousins —— eh, mother?"

"If you look at it that way! But a beaver muff would keep your hands warmer."

"Never mind! We 've got the candy, and I 'm going to sample it right away. Which will you have — buttercups or violets? Here 's all kinds," cried Martha, defying her plurals recklessly. "Nut-caramels — heavenly! And nougats, and fig-paste — real lumps of delight! Help yourself, mother! It 's no use denying that a box of candy is exciting," she rattled on. "Did I ever have one before? Oh, what is this, I wonder?"— as she spied a tiny box wedged between two candied apricots. "What do you think it is, mother? 'Something nice for Betsy Price'? But somehow,"— her eyes shining with a new excitement,— "it does n't look — exactly — like a sugar-plum."

"It looks much more like a ring," said Mrs. Redfield.

"And so it is. Why, *mother!*"

Martha's eyes grew round as moons, for the lid of the little satin-lined case had sprung open, and a lovely single pearl, set on a slim gold hoop, revealed itself.

"A pearl ring!" exclaimed Mrs. Redfield, equally excited. "Well, that *is* a surprise!"

Martha clasped her hands and rolled up her eyes like a tragedy queen. "The desire of my heart, the dream of my life!" she cried. "But it can't be true. I 'm asleep in the middle of a fairy-tale. I shall wake up in the moonlight with a cold in my head, and the pearl will be a pop-corn; I 'm sure of it!"

"Don't be silly," said her mother. "If it 's a fairy-tale, Cousin Jane is the fairy — as usual. Here 's her card."

She had found a slip of pasteboard with Cousin Jane's name on one side, and on the other, in her prim, old-fashioned writing:

Merry Christmas to my dear Cousin, with the hope that this little gift will prove useful and ornamental.

THE package addressed to Miss Mary Rutherford was left at a very different-looking place from the plain little home of the Redfields. It was a delightful old red-brick house set in the midst of vines and shrubbery, and its big, sunny parlor, full of books and pictures and flowers and singing-birds and easy-chairs, was equally unlike the Redfield sitting-room, with its faded carpet and well-worn furniture. The mother and daughter were different also. Mary Rutherford was only a year older than Martha, but she was taller and prettier and better dressed, and looked like a young lady, while Martha looked like a school-girl. She had soft, white hands that had never been roughened by work, and sweet, graceful manners that made you certain she had always been shielded from disagreeable things. In fact, she looked like one of the lilies that toil not, neither do they spin. And her mother had the same air of gentle refinement.

"What has Cousin Jane sent you, my dear?"—as the parcel was opened. "Something pretty, of course."

"Ye-s," was the daughter's rather hesitating answer. "Pretty enough, I suppose. It seems to be a sort of work-bag."

Mrs. Rutherford raised her eyebrows.

"A work-bag? How curious! Let me see it."

Mary handed it to her mother, and they inspected it together. It was quite large, and made of plum-colored silk with a sky-blue lining and satin drawing-strings. A circle of little pockets were each ornamented with a motto embroidered in blue floss, and inside were a number of working-implements,— scissors, thimble-case, emery-cushion, and darner,— all handsomely mounted in silver. The pockets were filled with papers of needles and spools of silk and thread. It was a completely furnished work-bag, in short, and thoroughly satisfactory — as a work-bag. But as a present it seemed to be a failure.

Mrs. Rutherford looked curiously at the mottos on the pockets.

"They seem to be very nicely worked," she said. "But I can't quite make them out. Can you?"

"Oh, yes, mama. One of them is, 'Never too late to mend.'"

"Very appropriate, I 'm sure."

"But rather pointed, don't you think, mama? Another is, 'A stitch in time save nine.' Does Cousin Jane think that I go in rags and tags, do you suppose?"

"Oh, it is only a decoration," said her mother. "It is the fashion nowadays to revive old-fashioned things."

"Here is one from the Bible," continued Mary. "'Whatsoever thy hand findeth to do, do it with thy might.' And here is another — from

Proverbs, is n't it? 'She worketh willingly with her hands.' It is a bagful of good advice. I dare say I needed it."

" Did Cousin Jane's card come with it?" asked Mrs. Rutherford. " Perhaps she did not send it, after all. It would be much more like Grandmother Darrow."

"Oh, no! Dear old Grandmother Darrow sent me a bead reticule — don't you remember? And here 's the card, besides:

> " Kindest love to my dear Cousin, and wishing she may
> always possess the pearl of great price.

What has the pearl of great price got to do with a silk work-bag, mama?"

" I 'm sure I don't know ! Unless she thinks that King Lemuel's is the only pattern for a perfect woman."

" It is not quite clear, even so," returned Mary. " But it is a handsome bag, at all events."

She took it quietly to her room, and no more was said about it. But in her heart she was mortified and disappointed. Cousin Jane's gifts to her, hitherto, had always seemed to confer, and imply, a sort of distinction. Her choicest books, the Parian statuettes on her mantel, the fine engravings that decorated her own room, the Florentine mosaics that were her prettiest ornaments — all these were tokens of Cousin Jane's good taste, and tributes to her appreciation of it. She had never sent her anything commonplace before; and far from expecting it on this occasion, Mary had dreamed of something still more individual and significant. It was only a word of Cousin Jane's, a smiling allusion to her pretty hands, that gave her the idea. " But I thought," said Mary, as her pretty hands hung up the bag — " I did think she meant to send me a pearl ring !"

In due time Cousin Jane, who had never suspected her mistake, received two letters of acknowledgment. The first, from Martha, was overflowing with gratitude :

How can I thank you enough, you dear, *dear* Cousin Jane, for your beautiful gift ? Ornamental ? I never had anything so ornamental before ! And useful, too, in a way that I feel better than I can express. How came you to guess at the wish of my heart ? It 's like a lovely dream come true. Thank you a thousand times, dear Cousin Jane, for your constant kindness to
Your grateful, affectionate   MARTHA.

The one from Mary Rutherford was cooler in its tone :

DEAR COUSIN JANE: Thank you very much for your kind gift. I hope it will help me to find "pearls of great price" — more than one of them, perhaps. I am ashamed to own that I have not been a diligent seeker after such treasure. But "it is never too late to mend," and some day I hope you will see that your suggestions have taken effect. With best love from mama and my brothers,   Your always affectionate cousin,

MARY RUTHERFORD.

These letters were rather puzzling to Cousin Jane. She read Mary's twice over, and laid it down with a sigh.

"I must say it is hardly what I expected from her," she soliloquized. "But poor little Martha is pleased, at any rate. She seems more delighted with her work-bag than Mary with her pearl ring. I took pains with that ring, too. It 's a very fine pearl, whether she knows it or not. She never even mentions the candy either, though I thought most girls were pleased with good candy in fancy boxes. Hopes I will see that my suggestions have taken effect — what does she mean by that, I wonder? I think I 'll have to write and ask her."

But Cousin Jane was not given to letter-writing, except on business. She had considerable correspondence of that sort, and many other ways of using her time; so she never wrote to Mary, after all. Some months later, however, she had occasion to visit the distant city where the Rutherfords lived; and after settling her business affairs, she went to spend the night with her cousins.

It was always pleasant to visit them, for she liked the atmosphere of the house. Mrs. Rutherford was a very gracious lady, gentle and kindly; her sons were well-bred, intelligent young men; and Mary, who had been a lovely child always, seemed to her now quite the ideal young girl, pure and fair as a lily, without and within. Secretly, Cousin Jane had always been a little sentimental about Mary Rutherford. She never said so to any one; but in her heart she loved her best of all the cousins.

That evening, as she sat alone with Mary in her own room, she thought the young girl looked more like a lily than ever. Mary had asked her to come in for a bedtime talk after she had said good night to the rest of the family; and Mary began to talk with a sweet seriousness that her cousin found charming.

"I 've been wishing for a long time to see you all by myself," she said. "There were too many things to write, and I never can write a letter that satisfies me, either. But I did want you to know how much a certain present of yours had done for me."

"Really? I wonder you don't wear it, then!" — for Cousin Jane had noticed with surprise that the pearl ring was not on her finger.

"I can't exactly *wear* it," Mary answered, surprised in her turn; "but it has been about with me a great deal, I assure you. And without vanity, I

"'DID COUSIN JANE'S CARD COME WITH IT?' ASKED MRS. RUTHERFORD."

think I can tell you that it has done a good work for an idle, self-indulgent girl."

"If you are the girl, I never heard you described by those adjectives," said Cousin Jane, warmly.

"Because every one has spoiled me. You were the first one to suggest to me that it was never too late to mend."

"That's news too," returned her cousin. "I never thought, myself, that you needed mending. What *do* you mean, child?"

"Why, the work-bag, you know. Don't you remember that beautiful silk bag, with the proverbs on the pockets, and the silver things inside? The card, too, with such a dear wish on it? Here it is, Cousin Jane, card and all. It has been my best friend ever since you sent it; though I am ashamed to confess that it was a disappointment — just at first."

She took the work-bag from its hook, as she spoke, and held it up before her cousin, who could hardly believe the evidence of her own eyes.

"What are you doing with Martha's bag?" was her astonished outcry. "I never sent that thing to you. I sent it to Martha Redfield."

"To Martha Redfield?" Mary repeated, dropping the bag in her bewilderment. "What do you mean, Cousin Jane? *Who* is Martha Redfield?"

"One of my cousins; at least, her father was. He is dead now, and she and her mother have none too much to live upon. Martha is in the high school, and means to teach as soon as she can."

"And you sent the work-bag to *her?* You meant the mottos for *her?* And the card too?"

"I never noticed that there were any mottos," said Cousin Jane. "I bought the bag at the Woman's Exchange. It looked strong and serviceable, and I knew Martha would have plenty of use for such a thing. I put the silver scissors, and so forth, inside, to make it a little more festive. As for the card,"— holding it up to the light and studying it through her spectacles,— "that has no business to be here. It should have gone with the pearl ring, of course."

"The pearl ring!" exclaimed Mary, catching her breath sharply.

"Certainly. The ring that I sent you in a box of candy."

"A box of candy, too? *Cousin Jane!*"

Mary sat down hastily, and stared before her with an unusual look in her face. Her hands clenched themselves in her lap; she bit her lips to crush back rising tears; and presently she laughed hysterically.

"I hope," she sobbed, unable to control herself any longer — "I hope Martha Redfield is happy with my ring! It was the thing I *wanted* you to

give me! And one does n't have a box of candy every day — but you like
a little — to offer your girl friends — "

She broke down with a sob; and Cousin Jane, seeing the truth at last,
cried out indignantly :

" You shall have another box to-morrow! And Martha shall send back
the ring. She might have known it was not meant for her! Never mind,
my dear. I suppose I must have made a stupid mistake. I 'm getting old,
child! But it won't take long to settle this business. I 'll stop and see
Martha on my way home to-morrow."

" No, no, Cousin Jane! *Please* don't!"

Mary pulled herself together with a brave effort.

" I could n't bear to have that done " — as she dashed away her tears.
"Just fancy how she would feel! Oh, I know by myself. Please *don't!* "

" But I meant it for you," protested Cousin Jane, clasping Mary's hand
and stroking it fondly. " This is just the dear little hand to wear pearls.
They suit it, and they suit *you*."

" How sweet to have you say so!" And Mary blushed with pleasure,
but persisted still : " Martha thinks you meant it for *her*, all this time; and
how mortifying it would be to have to give it up to another girl now! It was
foolish and babyish of me to cry about it. I am ashamed of myself. And
really I *could* n't take it from her. I should always feel as if I had robbed
her, and so would she. Besides," — with a sunshiny smile, and a squeeze
of Cousin Jane's hand,— " I should have to give up my beloved work-bag,
don't you see? And I can't possibly part with that. You listen now till I
tell you what a Moral Regenerator my bag has been."

There was a long talk after this — the sort of talk that girls pour out
sometimes to sympathetic older people who are not their mothers or sisters.
Cousin Jane discovered that, sweet and lily-like as Mary always was, she
had been in danger of growing up indolent, purposeless, even selfish ; and
that the work-bag and its pointed texts had opened her eyes to that fact.
The inference that things were different nowadays followed naturally. It
appeared that Mary's mother had been relieved of various household cares—
" all the mending, for instance!"—and that the Moral Regenerator had
been the leader in organizing a guild to work for the Children's Hospital,
where just such work was needed. Mary was very simple and modest about
it all, but very much in earnest, full of enthusiasm and self-forgetting interest.
Listening to her, Cousin Jane thought that putting one's heart into such
work might be one of the ways of seeking, and finding, " the pearl of great
price."

Late in the afternoon of another day, she stopped over a train, on her way home, to call upon the Redfields. She had faithfully promised not to speak of the mistake which had been made; but after this talk with Mary, she was curious to see if the ring had a story to tell as well as the work-bag.

"'I THINK I DID N'T WANT YOU TO SEE MY FACE,' MARTHA REPLIED,
SETTLING HERSELF ON THE HASSOCK."

Fortunately, Mrs. Redfield was not at home. Martha sat alone in the little parlor, studying her lessons between firelight and twilight; but she sprang up to greet her visitor with evident delight.

"Cousin Jane! You are the person I was wishing for just this minute. It's like a fairy godmother that comes when you think of her."

"Indeed? And why did you happen to think of a fairy godmother just now?" asked Cousin Jane, smiling as she took the easy-chair which Martha drew up to the grate for her.

"I don't know. I was trying to study my lessons, but the firelight kept shining on *this*,"—lifting up her ring-finger,—"and then I fell to thinking of you, and wishing I could tell you something."

"So you can, you see. I have come to listen to you."

"I see you have! And it truly is like a fairy godmother," cried Martha, her eyes dancing with happy excitement. "But it's been a sort of fairy-tale, you know, ever since I got my ring. Did you guess that it was going to make a real happy little girl, a real good little girl, out of crosspatch Martha?"

"Was n't she happy and good before?" asked Cousin Jane.

"Well—not much. Not always, anyhow."

Martha laughed, and poked the fire till the sparks flew up.

"You see, it comes easy to some girls to be angels," she continued; "but I'm not one of them."

"Comes easy?—why? Because their lives are easy?"

"Partly. It's easier to be good, of course, when you're comfortable, and you know your mother is n't worrying about the house-rent, or your winter clothes, or—'any old thing'! But some girls are good in spite of all that. They have been born sweet, you see, and trials only make them sweeter. Little Martha was n't cut by their pattern."

"What is Martha's pattern, then?" laughed Cousin Jane.

"She was cut on the bias, I'm afraid. And it made her pull the wrong way. She used to look at everything through blue glasses."

"Used to? And what does she do now?"

"She looks through a big, beautiful pearl," said Martha, gaily; "and it makes all the difference in the world."

"Suppose you tell me about it," returned Cousin Jane, very much interested. "I always liked the fairy-tale about pearls and toads."

"It is n't quite so bad as that! But still it's bad enough. May I sit on the hassock at your feet while I tell you? And do you mind not having the gas lighted?"

"Not at all. I can see your face by the firelight."

"I think I did n't want you to see my face," Martha replied, settling herself on the hassock. "But no matter. I'm going to make an honest confession."

"That 's always good for the soul, my dear."

"You 've been very good to mother and me, Cousin Jane. And my name is Gip," was Martha's beginning. "Only you have to spell it backward."

"Gip?" Cousin Jane looked puzzled. •

"Spelled backward," repeated Martha.

"Oh!" And Cousin Jane understood:

"Yes, just so! As I remarked, you 've been awfully good to us, and *mother* has been grateful. She has welcomed the new gowns, and the old ones to make over. She has blessed you, with tears in her eyes, for the checks that carried her through tight places. As for me, I 've said in my heart every time, 'Cousin Jane treats us like paupers, and we *are* paupers; but I hate it — I hate it — I hate it! I wish she would ever send us something that we *did n't* need.'"

"Oh!" said Cousin Jane again.

And Martha said, her cheeks red with honest blushes:

"Yes, just so! I was as mean as that, and I never, never deserved to be rewarded with this dear, lovely ring. But, all the same, it was a beautiful inspiration. What made you think of it, Cousin Jane? I wish you 'd tell me!"

"Impossible, my dear," replied Cousin Jane, remembering her promise to Mary. "Perhaps it was just a beautiful inspiration, as you say."

"It has been one to me, at all events. I don't know if I can make you understand, but it uplifted me, and it cast me down. It made me proud, and it made me ashamed."

"They were natural feelings," said Cousin Jane, kindly; "and both were wholesome."

"You think so? Oh, you *do* understand!" Martha exclaimed fervently. "How glad I am of the chance to talk it out with you! I 'm not a shining light yet — far from it. But whenever I look at this pearl, I think of what I *ought* to be, and it gives me some of the right kind of thoughts — it truly does."

"I 'm truly glad to hear it, Martha."

"I thought you 'd like to know that it puts a kind of pearliness into all my views of life. And, on the other hand," — with a twinkle of fun in her honest eyes, — "when the girls admire it, and envy me, it 's no use denying that I do feel kind of biggety."

"Biggety?" repeated Cousin Jane; and Martha laughed, and explained.

"A little toploftical, I mean. There is n't a girl in class who has anything to compare with my ring; and it does make me feel so — becoming to myself."

"You foolish child!"

But Cousin Jane liked the foolishness, and sympathized with the girlish confidences, which were different from Mary Rutherford's, but as natural and innocent in their way.

Mrs. Redfield came in by and by, and the gas was lighted, and Martha ran off to make a cup of tea for her visitor. Afterward she went down to the railroad station with her. And Cousin Jane thought, as she kissed her good-by, that her mistake had done no one any harm. On the contrary, it had shown her, as she might never have seen them otherwise, the true natures of two lovable girls.

SANTA CLAUS: "HERE 'S A STATE OF THINGS! HOW IN THE WORLD AM I EVER TO GET DOWN THERE?"

Ye Merrie Christmas Feast.

Ye Merrie Christmas Feast

by Edith M. Thomas

Now Grace is said, no longer wait,
With eyes downcast on emptie plate.
But see ye Turkey, fat, supine,
On which, good People, ye shall dine!
There lieth he,—a noble bulk,
That soone shall be a shattered hulk.
Carve, Goodman, carve, with speed and skill—
Ye Guests, spare not, but ete your fill!

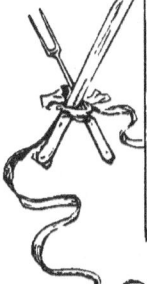

But who is this, that this way comes?
Sir Bagge-Pudding, with wealth of plums:
Ha! smell ye not ye savorie fumes?
Ye Orient on this table blooms.
Ye Tropics here their Dainties spill—
Ye Guests, spare not, but ete your fill!

Ye Merrie Christmas Feast

nd now come Junkets, Jumbles, Tartes,
And, after these, ye mince-meat Pie.
And monumental Cake, piled high.
Made by ye cunning Queene of Hearts
Who all surveys with beaming eye.
Quoth she: "Pray tarrie, tarrie still:
Ye Guests, spare not, but ete your fill!"

Ye Merrie Christmas Feast

e Feast is done. Ye Day is gone.
And Sleepe his curtains dark has drawn;
There through peepes many a fearful thing:
Ye Turkey and Ye Bagge-Pudding
On legges goe strutting up and downe;
Ye Mince-Pie weares a deadly frowne;
Ye Cakes and Jumbles lead a dance;
Ye Tartes and Junkets madly prance.
Because, O Guests, ye ate your fill.
These sprittes have now their evil will!

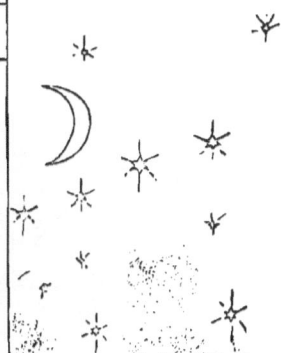

·SANTA·CLAUS'·PONY·

BY ELLA F. MOSBY

IT was a little town in Belgium. There were the storks' nests on the high red roofs to which the children pointed, as they pattered by in their little wooden shoes, or sabots; and there were small carts drawn by the strong draft-dogs of Flemish breed, looking at their owners with patient, faithful eyes. There were old churches and houses, telling a story in wood or stone to every passer-by.

In one of these old houses, built with queer gables and little balconies, and with a date and the name of the builder carved over the door, once lived two boys — Jan and Peter Stein. They were sons of a thrifty, honest Flemish burgher, who gave with an open hand to "God's poor," of whom there were very many after the sad wars of those days. There were so many, indeed, that the good burgher's own household lived very plainly, except at the joyous Christmas-time, when all Christians keep feast.

The children in Belgium have a charming Christmas legend about Santa Claus' pony. They always place their wooden sabots on the window-ledge, stuffed full of oats, hay, and fodder for the "dear Christmas pony." In the early morning they run on tiptoe to look; and behold! the hay is all gone, and the shoes are brimming over with toys and sweetmeats! Then the children clap their hands with glee, and wish they could only have waked in time to see the pony munching his oats. That would have been such fun!

Christmas week in Burgher Stein's household was one of great plenty; and not only every friend but every beggar that knocked at the side door had a share. There were black-puddings and liver-puddings, geese stuffed with chestnuts, and more than one noble turkey with truffles; and for at least a week beforehand was the little mother busy in the kitchen, mixing the rich Walloon wafers, that made little Peter's mouth water even when he happened to be thinking of them on a midsummer day.

Jan was four years and a half older than Peter, and he did not care so much either about the plain living all the year or the stuffed geese and wafers at Christmas; he wanted to go to school at the "Griffin House," as he called the old stone building carved with griffins and dragons for water-spouts and gargoyles and gable-ends, where they taught drawing and carving and architecture, as well as other things less delightful. Now he and Peter went to school to Captain Jacobi, who asked very little money, but also taught very little learning. How could he, when he had been fighting all the time until he lost his leg? If Jan had wanted, indeed, to hear about battles and sieges — but Jan's heart was set upon building up in stone and marble some of the fairy dreams he had in his brain. He loved even the queer old stone griffins on the school-house, with the quirks in their impossible tails. But the tender-hearted burgher could never keep money enough in his purse to send Jan there — certainly not to send both of his boys, and he and Peterkin had never been separated in all of Peter's short life. No; Jan's heart sank; it was altogether impossible.

"Go, boys," called their mother from the spicy, steaming kitchen — "go quickly and bring home the red cow. She has strayed away to the marsh; but be careful, boys; don't stay out after sunset. It is Christmas eve, remember."

As if they had forgotten it for one moment during the day! As if their Sunday sabots were not already arranged on the tall window-ledge, and filled with oats and hay and grass for the Christmas pony! To Peterkin's affectionate heart the Christmas pony was a wonderful and glorified creature. On summer holidays, when Santa Claus was busy in his workshop fashioning toys for winter delights, he imagined the white pony with its fiery, shining eyes and long waving mane and tail, as free, like himself, and enjoying many an untrammeled run and caper in a paradise pasture. Having once seen a picture of the Greek Pegasus, he confessed to his brother that he never thereafter thought of the Christmas pony without wings, though hidden, doubtless, to ordinary vision by his long, silvery mane. He believed firmly that one night he had actually heard him neigh softly, and paw at the wooden ledge.

Both the boys were restless,— "Christmas was in their bones,"— and so they ran with delight along the frozen path to the marshes to find "Kneidel," the strayed red cow.

The ground was so level that they could see all around them for a great distance ; and there, sure enough, was Kneidel, looking disappointedly at the withered grasses on the farther edge of the marsh. She seemed redder than ever in the glow of the sky, which was a deep red with a few dark clouds above like smoke.

"It looks like a goblin smithy," said Jan.

"Where they shoe with silver the Christmas pony," added Peter, laughing.

He put his hands on each side of his mouth to call Kneidel home, when a sudden sharp, ringing sound, as of hoofs striking on the frozen ground, made him pause, and around a small body of woods on one side of them came a little girl of thirteen or fourteen years riding a white pony, at the sight of which little Peter's breath came quick, and his cheeks flushed ; for had it not bright eyes, and long silky mane and tail, and was not the bridle shining with rich metal-work ?

Its rider, the young girl, drew rein and checked her pony's speed as soon as she saw the boys. Her eyes were black and lustrous, and her hair dark. She did not look like the girls of Flanders, nor was her dress like theirs ; and when she spoke it was with a decidedly foreign accent.

"You are Flemish boys, I see," she said, addressing Jan, and her voice was very sweet. "Can you tell me in what direction the castle lies? I thought it could be seen anywhere in this flat country."

"It is the old windmill that cuts off the view here," answered Jan ; "but after you cross the marsh yonder it is visible again. It is not far away."

"Then I will wait for the others," said the little lady, for so she seemed to be from her manner and look. "I was going to spend Christmas eve with my godmother,— at the castle,— and my father did not return. So, as I wished *very* much to go, the steward and the governess prepared to go with me, and they were so slow — oh, so slow ! — that my pony ran away and I find myself lost."

But there was a ring of mischievous laughter in the last sentence, and Jan shrewdly suspected that the pony was not altogether to blame.

"Is this the Christmas pony?" suddenly asked Peterkin, after an absorbed contemplation, for some moments, of the pretty white creature.

"Is it?—oh, yes, it is Santa Claus' pony!" she answered, with a merry glance at Jan, and eyes, lips, and dimples over-brimming with silent laughter. She evidently remembered the Flemish legend.

"Come," she said suddenly to Jan, with childlike impulse, "since I have to wait, tell me about yourselves; tell me what *you* would rather have —oh, of all things in the whole wide world! —for your Christmas gift!"

Children's hearts fly quickly open, and Jan was soon telling her, while she listened with wide, eager eyes, of his dream of going to the "Griffin House" and learning to build churches and

"A LITTLE GIRL RIDING A WHITE PONY, AT THE SIGHT OF WHICH LITTLE PETER'S BREATH CAME QUICK."

palaces; and how he could not do it, because he could never have the heart to rob "God's poor" of his father's aid in charity. Nor would he go without little Peter.

They were talking so eagerly that another rider was with them before they noticed his approach: a tall, dignified, dark-looking gentleman, wrapped in a long Spanish cloak and wearing a plumed hat. At the sight of him, and the sound of the young girl's rapturous cry, "Father!" Jan's lips closed, and a sullen and lowering look came over his frank face. He replied but curtly to their thanks, and turned to his brother. "Call Kneidel, Peter, and let us go home."

"Kneidel has gone, brother"; and so she had, like a sensible cow, mindful of supper and shelter; and the sunset fires of the winter sky were burned almost to embers.

They had separated, the young rider with a hurt, amazed look on her face, when Jan turned back and said to the gentleman : "Do not cross the marsh there. The holes are black and deep, and dangerous for horses. Take the longer road around. You will be at your goal the sooner — and the safer."

"You do not like to warn us," said the Spaniard, looking curiously at his half-averted, reluctant face. "Why?"

"Because you are Spanish," answered the lad, his honest gray eyes suddenly aflame.

"Who is your father?" questioned the Spaniard.

Jan's heart filled with dismayed apprehension. He remembered that he had told the daughter already, however.

"There is no need to tell," he answered sturdily. "I have not been treacherous to you, at least"; and his eyes sought the girl's eyes in warning.

She spoke quickly, in spite of a frown on her father's brow : "No; you have been a generous foe. We owe you only thanks."

There was a suspicion of tears about her long lashes, and Jan found it hard to listen to little Peter as they hastened homeward.

"It is strange she should have the Christmas pony," he was saying in a perplexed tone.

"Strange things always happen at Christmas," his brother answered dreamily.

Next morning a silken purse of gold pieces hung outside the window, with a scroll attached :

> For Jan and Peter Stein, that they may go to the School of the Griffins.
> From Santa Claus' Pony.

Jan Stein's desire was fulfilled. He and Peter went to the Griffin School and learned all about carving and building in wood and stone. They used to plan together what they would build as soon as they were grown : big churches, perhaps, and stately houses, but certainly a town hall for their own dear town, for the old one had been quite ruined by Spanish shells. Jan would have it adorned with pictures from its own history, and with carvings

THE SILKEN PURSE OF GOLD PIECES.

of familiar leaves and blossoms, and of common animals with their homely, every-day ways.

"The storks on their rough nests, and the big dogs harnessed to the cart — these would *I* have," said Jan.

"And the Christmas pony!" exclaimed Peter, his eyes kindling with the old enthusiasm. "On the central tablet would I carve him, and he should have wings, to show he is of no common stock, but of heavenly breed and nurture, and little panniers on his back out of which crowd all kinds of toys, and in front a child's sabots full of grass and barley. That should be my part, and under it would be only 'Peterkin' for the name of the carver."

"Why?" asked Jan, wonderingly, for this was only his home-name.

"Because I shall be always 'little Peter' beside you, brother!"

Peter took the greatest delight in thinking how great and famous Jan would be some day; and then, he thought, Jan would meet the little Spanish lady, and they would be true friends. Peter did not live to see Jan's success, for he died while they were students. But I think Jan did no work without writing under his own name that of "Peter Stein," since surely it was his brother's thought as well as his, though only Jan's hand carved it in stone.

The Wandering Minstrel

BY MARGARET HAMILTON

WHAT ho, within! Good honest
    folk,
  Here's one will sing you ballads
      quaint
  As carven shapes of fiend and saint
  That deck your beams of blackened
      oak.
  What ho, mine host! Here's one at
      last
  Who comes to solace all your guests
  With merry songs that made their
      nests
  Among the gables of the Past.

Then let him in; he knows the way
  To sweeten loaf and brighten fire;
  He sings of crested knight and
      squire,
Of lovely dame and friendly fay;
Of turbaned Paynims dark and fierce,
  Of elfin circles emerald green,
  Of blades by wizard art made keen,

And shields no mortal dart could
      pierce.

And though your coin must pay his
      pains,
  Not all for gold he plies his art,
  But holiday is in his heart
E'en while he stands and counts his
      gains.

To him should every door unbar
  At Christmas-tide; for then he
      sings
  Old chansons of the three wise
      Kings
Of Orient, and the mystic Star.
"Noël! Noël!" the carol rings
  Through cold blue night, afar, afar,
  And bears to cots where shepherds
      are
White thoughts that throng on angel-
      wings.

THE WANDERING MINSTREL

SANTA CLAUS IN TROUBLE.

The Bloom of the Christmas-Tree

BY MARY MAPES DODGE

AT night we planted the Christmas-tree
In the pretty home, all secretly;
All secretly, though merry of heart,
With many a whisper, many a start.
(For children who 'd scorn to make believe
May not sleep soundly on Christmas eve.)

And then the tree began to bloom,
Filling with beauty the conscious room.
The branches curved in a perfect poise,
Laden with wonders that men call "toys,"
Blooming and ripening (and still no noise),
Until we merry folk stole away
To rest and dream till dawn of day.

In the morning the world was a girl and a boy,
The universe only their shouts of joy,
Till every branch and bough had bent
To yield the treasure the Christ-child sent.
And then—and then—the children flew
Into our arms, as children do,
And whispered, over and over again,
That oldest, newest, sweetest refrain,
"I love you! I love you! Yes, I love *you!*"
And hugged and scrambled, as children do,
And we said in our hearts, all secretly:
"*This* is the bloom of the Christmas-tree!"

A Christmas-Eve Thought

BY HARRIOT BREWER STERLING

IF Santa Claus should stumble,
  As he climbs the chimney tall
With all this ice upon it,
  I 'm 'fraid he 'd get a fall
And smash himself to pieces —
  To say nothing of the toys!
Dear me, what sorrow that would bring
  To all the girls and boys!
So I am going to write a note
  And pin it to the gate,—
I 'll write it large, so he can see,
  No matter if it 's late,—
And say, " Dear Santa Claus, don't try
  To climb the roof to-night,
But walk right in, the door 's unlocked,
  The nursery 's on the right!"

SANTA CLAUS CAUGHT AT LAST.

A Christmas White Elephant

BY W. A. WILSON

FRED was in a sad quandary. There were certain things in the house which managed themselves, that is, were attended to by Agnes, his wife. There were others which required careful and judicious treatment, he said. These were left to him, of course. He found them, usually, more or less disagreeable. This case, however, was particularly difficult to deal with; the more so as it was plain to him that not only his own feelings, but those of Cecie, his little five-year-old daughter, had become involved. Now, he was much attached to his only child, and, whatever might happen to his own feelings, he objected to hers being wounded in any way. The situation, therefore, became more and more perplexing. As a natural consequence, he put off, from day to day, deciding what was to be done.

Agnes had expressed herself with her customary decision. "We simply cannot keep it in the house," she said, one evening when Fred went into the matter once for all.

"That is true," admitted her husband.

"Very well, then: we may as well get rid of it at once," she concluded.

"Yes, but how?" asked Fred, with an air of clinching the matter with a question she would find it difficult to answer.

"How? That is simple enough, surely."

"Don't see it."

"Why, open the door and put it out."

"Wh-a-at!" cried Fred, "and let it *die* in the yard?"

"Why, yes. You don't need to be so silly about it."

"Silly about it! Silly about it!! It's all very well to say 'silly' about it, but I could n't do it. I could n't sleep at nights. It's a good thing Cecie is not here to hear her mother."

"Really, Fred, it seems to me that you are driving matters a little too far," remarked Agnes, in a tone of great severity.

"Driving! That's not bad. I am not driving; I am being driven," said Fred, pleased, however, that he seemed to have the better of the argument.

"Well, I don't know," she said. "You agree that it cannot stay, and yet you object to letting it go."

"I do nothing of the kind," said Fred, helplessly. "I only said it was n't feasible. It simply cannot be put out to die. It does n't cost much to feed it, you must admit."

"That is true," said Agnes; "but that has nothing to do with it. Surely there is no use going over all the reasons again."

"Then," said Fred, in desperation, "let us get a man to take it out into the country somewhere and leave it to its fate. Perhaps some one would take a fancy to it," he added, rising.

"That would cost more than it is worth. Besides, it is a good thing Cecie is not here to hear her father," laughed Agnes, and the subject was allowed to drop once more.

Fred felt that the matter was becoming serious. If Agnes were so unreasonable, what would Cecie say to a proposal to turn her newly found friend out of doors? If it had only not been so very large!

Cecie had become quite a personage of importance in the household. Her father was reminded so often of himself by things she said and did that he strove in every way to protect her from being, as he called it, badly used — that is, from being misconstrued and misunderstood. A strong feeling had, consequently, grown up between them. This case, this Green White Elephant of a Christmas-tree, was a characteristic instance. Only Cecie could have caused such a fuss about such a trifle. The more he thought about it the more ridiculous it seemed. Yet, as he said, it was easier to laugh than to say what was to be done.

Toward the end of the previous month, Robin, a friend, having sent a present consisting of a large Christmas-tree growing in an earthen pot, Fred went into town — unknown, of course, to Cecie — to purchase decorations for it. The same evening that young lady, having danced about the house all day and feeling tired, begged her father to read to her, as she expressed it, a nice fairy-tale. Fred was an artist, and had been occupied for some months illustrating a new edition of Hans Christian Andersen. He took up an old volume of his fairy-stories and opened it at random. It chanced that he stumbled upon the story of "The Fir-tree." This, as it happened, had not yet been read to his daughter, and as her father prepared to read he noticed that she settled herself on her stool at her mother's feet, and elaborately smoothed her pinafore out before her, as she was wont to do on great occasions; for no occasion was so great to Cecie as the first reading of a new fairy-tale.

He did not stop to think. It did not occur to him precisely what the result of reading that particular story at that particular time would most likely be. Otherwise, he would probably have kept it for another day. But he did not; he read innocently on, and Cecie listened. When he had finished she surprised him by saying nothing. She sat quite still, and seemed to have become very thoughtful. After a time she rose and went quietly into the room where the Christmas-tree was standing.

Presently a small voice called out: "Papa!"

Fred, suspecting what had happened, rose and went in. Agnes remained. She had an important piece of sewing to do.

"Papa," asked Cecie, whose blonde curls scarcely reached the lowest branches of the tree, "it never moves, does it?"

"No, dear."

"And it is alive just like us?"

"Yes. That is — well, yes; not exactly, you know, but it is quite alive."

"What does it feed on all the time, then?"

"The juices of the earth," said Fred, with the air of an experienced gardener. "That is why we must give it water. It requires air, too, for it sucks moisture in with these as well." And he pinched the branch nearest him, and a few needles came off between his fingers.

"Does n't that hurt the tree?" cried Cecie.

"Oh, no; it won't mind that."

"Would n't it like some juices just now, papa?"

"I think not. The earth is moist enough."

"Oh, let me! I 'll go and get some water," said Cecie, starting toward the door.

"No, no; it has sufficient."

"But perhaps it would like a long drink. I do, sometimes," pleaded the little girl, in tones which usually had the desired effect.

"No!" said the head of the family, to satisfy himself that he could be firm occasionally.

There was a pause. Cecie stood still, looking up at the handsome stranger as if she had never seen a tree before. "Do you think it hears us talking about it, papa?" she said after a moment.

"Perhaps."

"Perhaps it is asleep," she suggested, moving closer to her father and putting her little hand in his.

"Perhaps it is," said Fred, feeling that, after all, the tree might as well have had some water.

" But how does it sleep when it has no eyes?"

" Oh, it just sleeps in its own way."

" Standing up like that always?"

" Yes, just as, just as — let me see — as horses do, for example."

"Oh, but horses don't always," retorted Cecie; because the baker had told her, the other day, that his horse lay down on the straw and went to sleep whenever it got home at night.

"They sometimes do," observed Fred, in the interests of parental authority, meaning at the first opportunity to get reliable information on the subject of the private life of horses.

" Then will it like to live with us?"

Fred thought it would, if they were kind to it.

" And we will be kind to it, won't we?"

"Of course we will," Fred promised, in the innocence of his heart; for he was a child of nature himself, fond of flowers and trees and everything that lived a free and healthy life.

Then Cecie said good night to her tree, "and pleasant dreams"; and when she had closed the door for the night and left her new friend alone, she went contentedly away with her nurse; and Fred sat down, blissfully unconscious that he had committed himself in any way.

The following forenoon, after struggling for an hour to get into his work, Fred had just got fairly settled when he was startled by a fall, a crash of crockery, and a loud wail in the room adjoining his studio. Laying down his drawing-board and pen, with a sigh, he went to the folding doors and opened them.

Cecie had already been picked up. She was standing like a little model for a statuette, holding out her limp and dripping hands. Her pinafore and dress were soaked with water, and there was a pond on the bright waxed floor, dotted with islands of broken stoneware jug. The cat, in the center of the farther room, was excitedly licking its back. Cecie's lips were puckered up in great distress, and her eyes were lost in a spasm of tears, for she had startled no one more than she had herself.

Fred could not help smiling. He bent down and comforted her, and, after the tears had ceased, said that to prevent confusion in future, either he or mama, or at all events nurse, would see that the tree got sufficient water. Cecie was to give herself no concern whatever. There was no need to trouble herself about it. Would she be good and not do so any more?

"Y-y-yes," promised Cecie, feeling, however, that she was promising away her entire interest in life.

"Oh, I will tell you," said Fred. "Every evening at tea-time remind me that the tree is thirsty. Nurse can fetch us water, and we can give it some."

Cecie was led away for a change of clothes, with an expression on her face like sunshine breaking through the clouds on an April day. Fred, with a reflection of it glistening in his eyes, went back to his room and took up his board.

That evening he was busy decorating the tree for some time after Cecie had gone to sleep.

THE next evening was Christmas eve; but when the happy moment arrived, and the doors were flung open, disclosing the tree in a blaze of light, Cecie did not seem to rise to the occasion quite so enthusiastically as her parents had expected; and yet this was not only the largest but the finest tree she had ever had. Cecie, however, was not one who could be gay to order; and with her the unexpected usually happened. This time it was not that she did not think her protégé beautiful. She was divided between admiration and another feeling. She was wondering if it would care to be lighted up with candles within an inch of its life like that, and covered with glittering ornaments till it could scarcely breathe; whether it liked to have molten wax run all over its fresh green branches; and whether it were being treated with proper respect in being made to hold up such a load of things.

Fred laughed heartily when she confided her anxieties to him, and said, "Oh, that won't matter. Don't mind that, little woman."

"But don't you remember that the story said when the trees had bark-ache it was as bad as headache is to us?"

"Oh, but it is strong," said her father. "It does n't feel such little things."

"Well, I would have barkache — headache, I mean," said Cecie, laughing at her slip, "if I had to carry all those burning candles."

Later, when the little party had broken up and Fred was left alone, he sat down in an easy-chair. A question had occurred to him while Cecie was speaking. This tree of hers — what was to be done with it when its time came?

He and mama had no means of disposing of it, living in the city as they did, and it could not be kept in the house. Moreover, Cecie would require to know what had been done with it. Previous Christmas-trees had had their death-blows dealt them in the forest. With this one it was different. It was not only still living, but, thanks to Cecie, was becoming from day to day more and more a personality in the house.

Parents, he reflected, really ought to remember to tell their children, when talking of the duty of kindness to all dumb creatures, that there are exceptions to every rule — that is to say, if they wish to avoid drifting into ridiculous situations. To think of the father of a family hesitating about such a paltry thing as this! He looked up at the moment, and his eyes fell upon the tree. How beautiful it certainly was, in spite of all the finery and tinsel! Cecie was an odd child! However, when Christmas was over, other things would distract her attention, he hoped, and then it would be time enough to — well, that could be determined when the time came. Perhaps something would turn up before then.

"CECIE WAS DEEPLY ENGROSSED IN AN ILLUSTRATED SPELLING-BOOK."

THE next day, being Christmas, was a holiday. Fred sat reading in his easy-chair before the studio fire. Cecie, not far away, lay upon the floor, propping her head up with her arms, deeply engrossed in an illustrated spelling-book.   For a few moments there was no sound but the grave beat of the old timepiece hanging on the wall and the nervous ticking of two modern clocks in the adjoining room.   A thin fall of snow had slid down the studio windows and collected at the bottom of the panes.

Presently Fred laid down his book, and said, over his shoulder: "Where is Dolly to-day?"

"She's asleep just now," she said, rising and going to her father's side. "She's been making plum-pudding."   Taking the watch from her father's pocket, and holding it sideways, she continued: "What time is it?"

"A quarter past three."

"But you said it was twelve when the hands were together."

"Yes; but when they are together at the *top*."

Cecie gave it up.   Replacing the watch, she said, in an altered tone of voice: "Papa!"

"Well, dear?"

"Trees don't care for anything but growing, do they?"

"Well, I don't know that they care much even for that.   They have to grow just as you, just as I, must do."

"Must you grow, papa?"

"I?   Well, I suppose I am done growing now," said Fred.

"Will you never grow, never any more?" asked Cecie, so seriously that her father turned around and looked at her, and smiled.

"Well, dear," he said, stroking her hair, "it would n't do, you know, if we never stopped.   Think how big we should get to be!"

Cecie burst into a gay laugh.   "We could n't get in by the door, unless we bent down and crept in on our hands and knees, could we?"

"Of course we could n't," laughed Fred.

"But it is funny, too, that we have to stop growing.   Tell me, papa," she continued, looking earnestly at him, "are you *very* old?"

"Who?   I?" said Fred, aghast.   "No — of course not.   I am quite young."

"How old is old, then?"

"Old?   Let me see.   Fifty is old, or sixty — thereabouts," said Fred. After a silence Cecie began again:

"Will *I* ever be old, papa?"

"Why, certainly, my dear," said Fred, cheerfully; "that is," he added, as if feeling guilty of some vague ungallantry, "I hope so."

"And never grow any more, like you?"

"Y-yes."

"But would n't you like to keep growing always?"

"I don't know. I feel pretty comfortable as I am. If I were a little girl like you it might be different."

"Do people only want to grow when they are young?"

Fred shifted in his chair, and then, drawing her closer to him, said: "Why do you ask about the tree caring to grow?"

"Because you read in the story that the tree said to itself: 'Let me grow, only let me grow; there is nothing so beautiful in all the world.'"

"I don't remember."

"Wait, and I will get the book," said Cecie.

She returned with the volume, which she had opened at the proper place, and declared that it was at the very beginning.

"How did you know that that is the place?"

"Because the picture of the tree is there," replied the child, simply.

Fred patted her on the cheek, and ran his eye rapidly down the page. At length he said:

"Oh, yes; you are right. Here it is:

"'Be happy,' said the Sunshine, 'that you are young. Rejoice in your growth, and in the young life that is within you.' And the Wind kissed the tree by day, and the Dew wept over it by night: but the Fir-tree did not understand."

"What did n't it understand?" asked Cecie.

"Oh, I don't know," said her father, carelessly.

"I know."

"What, then?"

"That some day it would stop growing, like you, and might want to grow some more, and could n't," cried Cecie, breaking into a dance of joy; for she had a great belief that her father knew nearly everything, and it was a great treat to her to be able to tell him something he did not know.

Finally, as if by way of further relieving her feelings, she caught up one foot, and hopped round the studio and out at the open door.

As she did so, Fred's book slipped from his knee and fell. He picked it up again, but laid it on the table. Resuming his chair, he sat for some time with his head resting on his hand, looking absently at the fire.

CECIE sometimes had fits of not knowing what to do with her limbs; or it might, perhaps, be more correct to say that her limbs had fits of not knowing what to do with themselves and her. At one moment she would be seen lounging about like a marionette, hanging on her father or mother or whoever happened to be near. The next minute she had gone. She was

"THE TREE WAS CEREMONIOUSLY AND MOST DELICATELY WATERED, TO THE COMPLETE
SATISFACTION OF ITS PATRONESS."

likely, however, to reappear at any moment, like a kitten, the innocent victim
of some strange galvanic power.

These moods had the additional peculiarity of usually occurring when
every one else was disposed to be quiet. This occasion being no exception,

Fred was soon startled from his reverie by warm lips sending a sudden
" Boo-o-o ! " near his ear.

"What 's the matter?" he cried out, twitching as if from an electric
shock.

Cecie applied her lips to his ear again.

" I don't know," he said, laughing, and rubbing that organ energetically.

" Guess ! "

" Can't.   There is n't anything forgotten."

" Oh, yes, there is," said Cecie, and whispering a second time.

" Oh, not just now, I think," said Fred, smiling, as she retreated a pace
to watch the effect of the joyful communication.

" But you said you would."

" It won't require any water to-day."

" Oh, yes.   You know it has all the candles and things to hold."

Fred rose resignedly, and went into the room, and the tree was ceremoniously and most delicately watered, to the complete satisfaction of its
patroness.

It was large enough, certainly (its top just touched the ceiling of the
room in which it stood), but it was very kind of Robin, Fred reflected, to
have sent such a handsome tree.   If, therefore, this newly born enthusiasm
of Cecie's for growing were to be encouraged, it might soon be necessary
to take her friend into the studio.   But that was entirely out of the question.
He could not afford the space.   Sooner or later he must come to a decision.
There seemed to be no resource but to break it up for fire-wood.   Cecie
could be sent for a walk while that was being done.   Who was to do it, however?   It was not work for his wife, and he — well, he did not care to do it.
He was not accustomed to use an ax, for one thing; besides, work of that
sort was bad for an artist's hands.

Nurse would do it.   Why not?   She was a great, strong woman.

It was not until the first week of the new year, when the mistletoe and
holly and other relics of Christmas were being cleared away, that the subject of their silent visitor came up again.

" If Cecie would only tire of it," he would say to himself at times, " or if it
would only die !"   Of the latter, unfortunately, there seemed to be very little
prospect, unless, indeed, it died by drowning.   Thanks to Cecie's watchful-
ness, there seemed a distant possibility of that.

Once he pulled himself together, and, without daring to address himself
directly to his daughter, spoke about the matter, in a seemingly casual manner, in her presence.

"What shall we do when the tree is away?" he said to mama.

"It is n't going away, is it, papa?" asked Cecie, looking up in great surprise.   "You said it was to be allowed to stay."

"C-certainly, my dear.   I mean, what would we have done if it had been going away?"

Cecie's calmness had quite disarmed him.

"Where could it have gone, poor thing?" asked Cecie, tenderly.

"I — don't — know," said Fred, hopelessly.

Again he and Agnes were talking obscurely about it, so that the child might not understand.

Presently Cecie said in a low whisper:

"S-sh, mama, s-sh!   Don't talk like that.   The tree might hear you, and think you were talking about *it.*"

"But, my dear," said her mother, seizing the opportunity, "we *are* talking about it."   Suddenly lowering her voice, in response to an expression in Cecie's face, she added: "Something must be done, you know.   It cannot stay here always."

"Then," said Cecie in a hoarse whisper to her father, who had begun to crumble bread upon the table-cloth, "why did you let it hear you say it could, papa?"

"Me, dear?   I did n't."

"Yes, you did; the first night it came," persisted Cecie, her eyes filling suddenly.

"Did I?   Well, but we don't need to chop it up, you know," said Fred, soothingly.

"Chop it up!" cried Cecie, horrified.   "Who said we would chop it up?"

"Why, why — nobody.   Did nurse say so?"

"Nurse?   Why, no.   She loves it as much as I do now, ever since I told her," said Cecie.

"Oh!   I did n't know," said the victim, feeling that the toils were closing around him, and beginning to wonder if Hunding found it inconvenient to have a tree growing through the roof of his abode.   It might look picturesque, at least, if the worst came to the worst.

"Poor thing!" said Cecie, turning to their helpless charge; "we promised to be kind to you, and we will, won't we?"

Neither Fred nor Agnes said a word.   They felt that their best course was to wait.

Cecie, however, made it difficult for them at the outset by saying good night to her tree that evening with even more kindliness in her voice than usual.

Fred complained to Agnes afterward, as they sat alone together, that it was impossible to work when one was constantly distracted by the small things of life. Agnes said, "Stuff and nonsense!" Moreover, she added, laughing, it was absurd to call Cecie's tree a small thing of life. It was already too large, and, what was worse, seemed to be growing larger.

It was no wonder, therefore, that Fred was in a great quandary.

Whenever he chanced to see the tree, standing on its stool, so submissive or so indifferent,— he could not quite make out which,—but certainly so undeniably fresh and healthy-looking, his conscience gave a twinge. He began to avoid the "prison," as Agnes jestingly called the room in which it stood; for when he met the tree face to face, he always thought of the Good Robber, and how he must have felt when he took the Babes by the hand and led them to the Wood; and when he heard nurse watering it and spraying its branches twice a day, he winced, for he had delegated the work to her in the steadfast hope that she would forget to do it.

Once, with a bitter remembrance of this, he said to Agnes, who had complained of her neglect: "Yes; she does nothing she is told to do, that girl."

"Oh, papa," broke in Cecie, who happened to be in a corner of the room, "you can't say that. Look at the way she keeps the tree. Why, there are buds upon it already!"

At another time, Agnes, who had just decided to take the law into her own hands, and give orders for the execution without saying anything either to Cecie or her husband, was busy arranging her bookcase, when Fred looked up from the letter he was writing and said: "S-sh! Who is that in the next room?"

"It is only Cecie."

"But she is talking to some one."

Agnes laid down the book she was dusting, and, going softly to the door, stood still and listened. As she did so, a curious look, that was half smile and half something else, crossed her face.

"They are having a great time in there," she said in a lowered tone, coming away from the door. "Cecie is telling it a long story about a walk she had in the park with nurse."

Agnes resumed her work among the books, and decided that in the meantime there was no hurry; the tree could remain where it was for a day or two longer.

At last, at the eleventh hour, quite unexpectedly, a solution of the difficulty arrived.

13*

ONE windy night toward the end of January, Fred was awakened by the slamming of the folding windows in a room down-stairs.

He lay, reluctant to rise, for some moments, but, on the noise being repeated, sprang out of bed and put on his slippers.

Passing the staircase window like a ghost, he reached the hall, and moved toward the parlor door. The shutters were closed, and the room was dark. After feeling about, and upsetting a vase of water filled with flowers, and a few glasses and ornaments on a table, he succeeded in finding the matches, and struck a light.

He opened the door of the room whence the noise was coming; but, as he did so, the window was blown wide open, his lamp was extinguished, and he found himself in an almost forgotten presence.

Majestic and calm, within a few paces of him, stood the tree, in the great flood of moonlight which streamed in past the fluttering curtains.

Fifteen seconds later, Fred had shuffled up the staircase, and was coiled up in his bed again.

He told Cecie in the morning.

The tree's old friends had missed it, she said, and had come to pay it a visit to see how it was getting on.

" What *friends* ?" asked Frederick-of-the-Guilty-Conscience.

"The moonlight and the wind," said Cecie.

" Oh," said Fred.

That this little episode impressed Cecie was evident; but it was not until the following Saturday that she said anything of an idea which it seemed to have suggested to her. It was the first time since New Year's that Fred had found time to run out beyond the city, which he was in the habit of doing as often as he could, to spend a few hours in the pure, fresh air of his favorite woods. Agnes usually accompanied him, and, for the first time, they yielded to Cecie's entreaties and took her also with them.

These snatches of health-giving air, these walks, short though they were, on the country soil, were everything to Fred. Two hours of freedom among the trees, in the silence of the forest, he used to say, were enough to clear a week's cobwebs from the brain. They did more for him that day — they solved the problem of the tree.

To reach their favorite walk it was necessary to go by steamboat to a station down the river, and thence climb a short, steep hill to a wood which stretched for miles beyond. It was apt to be dusty and less attractive in the summer months, but in late autumn and winter and early spring, when deserted by the picnicking crowd, it was a beautiful and peaceful spot. The favorite corner of Fred's was a small pond which lay in the midst of a thicket

of young elms and oaks. When Cecie saw this for the first time she remained very quiet for some moments. Two fir-trees growing at a corner of the pond seemed to attract her attention.

"WHY NOT SEND OUR TREE OUT HERE AND LET IT GROW BESIDE THE OTHERS?"

"What are you thinking about?" asked her father.

"I am thinking — why not send our tree out here and let it grow beside the others? Look at those two poor trees standing over there, all alone. It would be happier too, I think. It would like to be beside them."

"Do you think it would?" asked Fred, musingly.

"I am sure of it!" cried Cecie, excitedly. "It would get the dew, and the wind, and the rain, and the sun, and could grow and grow all the time. I am afraid it won't grow much with us."

An hour afterward they stood on the pier watching their steamboat coming up the river.

"Now," said Fred, who seemed to be in unusually good spirits, "we have only to ask Robin if he is willing."

"Willing — what to do?"

"To let us send his present into the woods to live, instead of keeping it ourselves," said Fred, quite gravely.

"Oh, he will," said Cecie, confidently. "I will go and ask him. Nurse can take me — to-morrow morning — before breakfast-time."

"I think I would n't go quite so soon," said her father, with an amused look. "Robin does n't — I mean Robin is very busy in the early mornings."

The snow and ice had disappeared from the streets and avenues, and in the mild skies of the early days of February there was a glad respite from the cold, and a welcome promise of the coming spring.

The sun no longer hid behind banks of fog, but rose from day to day with clear and lustrous face. The mists had gathered up their trains and fled, and the skies were filled with armies of fleecy clouds. The grass in the parks seemed already to feel the breath of April, the crocuses peeped out from their beds of earth and hurried on their yellow garments, while the trees donned a livery of tiny buds and stood in sleepy readiness for the festival. The busy steamers plying up and down the river became suddenly gay with color; for the passengers no longer huddled together in heated cabins, but crowded out upon the deck that they might breathe the fresh air.

Beyond the city, nature seemed less eager to listen to fair promises, for her landscapes lay still as they had been left by the marauding winds of winter. The country roads were bleak and bare, the shrubs and hedges stripped of their leaves and left stifled with snow and mud, and the deserted foot-paths wandered listlessly through the maze of trunks and branches and lawless thorns. Yet when the sun shone into the thickets and down upon the inert ground, everything seemed to quicken: the ice retreated into the shady corners of the ponds, the drowsy trees lazily stretched themselves, and here and there in the recesses a bird took courage and began piping feeble snatches of almost forgotten song.

On the afternoon of one of these early February days the deserted woods seemed quieter even than they had been in the dead of winter. There was not a breath of wind to ruffle the surface of the pond, beside which a young fir-tree had recently been planted. Far in the distance a

dog's bark or a cock-crow might be heard; still farther, perhaps, a long, faint whistle from a train winding along the river's bank; or, nearer at hand, the rustle of a falling leaf; but these only served to make the silence more profound. Close beside two other firs, standing in friendly reserve some-

"'I SUPPOSE MISSY WILL BE SATISFIED NOW.'"

what aloof from the attendant herd of young oaks and elms, the new member of the mute community depended its lustrous green reflection into the

somber mirror at its feet.   Behind it rose the slender stems of two
silver birches.   In a corner near at hand a marsh-willow had burst into a
mist of downy buds; and, still nearer, an old oak, as if to show an example to the younger members of its family, who still clung to their tattered
covering of leaves, stretched its bare and rugged limbs far up above its
neighbors, and stood, stern and weather-beaten, on its carpet of grass and
fallen acorns.

The mossy foot-path which skirted the pond led to a clearing in the wood
where it joined a broader way.   This crossed a more open tract of ground
covered with bushes and clogged with heather and dark-leaved brambles,
until at one corner the country road appeared from behind a clump of trees.
Between this corner and the point, some distance farther on, where the road
descended the wooded hill leading to the river, a gardener's cottage was
situated.

At the gate of this cottage, toward sunset on a February afternoon, three
figures were standing.   The one in colored shirt-sleeves and ample cordu-
roys wore a gardener's blue apron; the others were clad in the more con-
ventional clothing of the city.

One of them wore a dark hat and cloak, and beside him stood a little
figure dressed in a quaint gown of blue trimmed with sable.   From beneath
the felt and feathers of her hat one of her blonde curls escaped and lay grace-
fully upon her shoulder.

A fourth figure, that of the gardener's wife, a motherly looking woman in
a faded cotton dress, presently disappeared into a small greenhouse near the
cottage, and closed the door behind her.

"Well," said the owner of the blue apron, in an affable tone, to his visitors, when at length they prepared to leave, "I suppose Missy will be satisfied now."

"I think so," said the figure in the cloak, looking down to "Missy," who
smiled a shy assent.   "*I* certainly am very well satisfied," he added, with a
quizzical look, while buttoning his cloak.

When they set out, a few minutes later, the sun was glittering behind
the trees, the earth was deep in color, and the sky was filled with light.

They had reached the point where the road dipped suddenly in the direction of the steamer-pier, when the door of the greenhouse opened, and the
woman with the faded gown reappeared, tying up a bouquet as she walked
slowly into the garden.

She did not look up at first, but when she did so and found that the
strangers had gone, she threw her scissors down upon a table, ran past her
husband, who was at the gate, and hastened after them along the road.

They turned on hearing her, and when she reached them she bent down and, with a mixture of hesitancy and tenderness, placed the flowers between two small gloved hands, and retreated.

A minute afterward she was standing in the middle of the empty road, bareheaded, and with cheeks hot and flushed, watching a waving cloak and a little dot of blue gradually disappearing down the avenue.

A CHRISTMAS DINNER.

Osman Pasha at Bucharest

(DECEMBER 25, 1877)

BY HELEN THAYER HUTCHESON

IN Servian hearths the Christmas fire
Did slowly molder and expire.
In Servian hearts there glowed a flame
No time shall quench, no tyrants tame.

Through royal Petersburg the Czar
Rode in his slow, triumphal car;
The Christmas bells rang loud and sweet
Before the Liberator's feet.

At Bucharest, where snow lay white
Beneath the friendly veil of night,
Was ushered in, with captive state,
The vanquished of the Czar and fate.

His brow was stern — on Plevna's plain
The snow fell fast upon the slain.
The Prophet's standards fled to sea;
Roumania — Servia — they are free!

Roumania's daughter, unaware,
Had caught the glance of stern despair;
She smiled on him with childish grace,
The vanquished tyrant of her race:

[This poem recounts an incident at the time of the Russian victory which liberated Christian Servia and Roumania from Moslem rule. Osman Pasha commanded the Turks in the defense of Plevna during the war between Russia and Turkey. Though Plevna was taken, he had shown himself so brave and skilful as to win the admiration even of his enemies. While Osman was a prisoner, and on his way through Bucharest, the capital of Roumania, a little Roumanian girl, touched by his dejected expression, ran forward and placed a flower in the hand of the defeated general.]

For comfort in this bitter hour
She laid within his hand a flower;
The captive's eyes with tears were dim,
He kissed the lips that smiled on him.

Sweet pledge of peace, and debt confessed
Between oppressor and oppressed!
An echo thrilling Moslem pride:
" Good will to men at Christmas-tide."

The Crescent wanes — the Star ascends —
The reign of force and terror ends;
And love hath overcome the sword
Upon the Birthday of the Lord.

A Snow-Bound Christmas

BY FRANCES COLE BURR

MOST of the occupants of the small room sat gazing out of the windows into the snow-filled air. There were windows enough to go around, though the room was long and narrow, and contained six or eight persons. All day they had spent together in this one room, each sitting quietly in his place. There had been but little conversation. The tall dark man with the white mustache and tired face had slept much, with his head resting on his folded overcoat. A boy opposite, who showed sullen anger and defiance in every line of his young face, had watched him, and wondered how a man could sleep in the daytime. The boy did not know that those long, nervous white hands, wielding a surgeon's knife, had saved a life the day before, and the tired eyes had watched for many hours following. An earnest, bright-faced young girl near by had observed him, too, while he slept, as she eyed all her neighbors, with keen interest. There was the old lady in the corner, a man with sample-cases piled at his side, the shabby little woman holding a big baby, and a middle-aged man with stolid, joyless countenance, who had read three newspapers through from beginning to end without a change of expression, and since then had sat staring straight before him. The girl in her active mind had tried to combine these various personages into a story, but she gave it up with a little sigh for their commonplaceness.

An ill-assorted company it was. Surely they would have chosen to spend the day before Christmas together for no other reason than, as it happened, they all wished to travel over this branch road, which ran between the northern line from Little Falls and the Grand Central.

The day was nearly over, and the journey should have been ; but the snow, which had been falling steadily since morning, grew heavier, the speed of the train perceptibly decreased, and the engine groaned and labored. The engineer watched apprehensively as they drew near a certain cut, narrow and deep, through the hills. It was drifted high; and meeting that soft, still, resistless opposition, the great engine slowed and stopped.

The drifting snow hid the familiar landmarks, and so it happened that, just as the passengers were anxiously questioning one another as to the cause of the stop in that lonely place, Jim Case, the fireman, swinging himself off the engine, slipped over a culvert, and in the fall of only a few feet broke his arm with startling ease and completeness. He was lifted back, white and fainting; and when the brisk conductor hurried into the passenger-coach, he responded to the anxious queries with a brief "Snowed up," and then, addressing the dark man, he said:

"I don't suppose you 're a doctor, are you?"

"Yes," said the man, with an inquiring glance; "does some one need me?"

The conductor looked relieved.

"Now, ain't that luck?" said he. "Surgeon, too, I guess?"

The doctor nodded assent.

In a few words the conductor told of the accident, amid exclamations of mingled sympathy and dismay from the listeners. And as the doctor picked up his small black bag and followed him into the forward car, the conductor continued:

"Not many of you travel on this road, but I thought that was your trade when I took your ticket. I gave a job to a surgeon once when I was hurt in a wreck. That was a good while ago, but I have never forgot the look or the feel of his hand — so steady and strong and white," he added, with an apologetic smile.

"Here we are, Jim!" he called out cheerily; "here is the doctor and the head nurse. You just break your bones, and we will do the rest, you know."

The fireman lay stretched upon the floor, his head resting languidly on a pile of waste, and a pretty five-year-old boy sobbing with fright was kneeling close beside him.

"Who is this little fellow?" asked Dr. Carleton, after the examination was over, and he was skilfully bandaging the injured arm.

"He 's mine, poor little chap!" said the fireman, with a tender glance, though his lips were white with pain.

The boy, who was a sturdy little fellow just out of dresses, stopped his sobs as he heard his father's voice, and looking up at the doctor, asked:

"Now will we go to grandma's, and have a Christmas?"

The man winced again, and closed his eyes; and the conductor explained in a kindly aside:

"Little chap's mother is dead: just buried her a week ago. She had him filled up choke-full of Christmas, and seems as if he could n't give it up. They are going on to Jim's mother's,— she 's going to take care of Jamie,— and I guess the old lady had promised to have a tree."

Jamie was listening eagerly, and broke in, forgetting his shyness:

"Yes; a Christmas-tree and candles; for grandma said so."

"Seems as if that is all he thinks of," said the fireman; "his poor mother — she —" and he stopped, and closed his eyes again.

"Shall we go now?" insisted Jamie. "You said that we 'd get there the night before Christmas."

"Now, young fellow," broke in the conductor, "you know this is road luck. You are a railroad man, and must learn to keep a stiff upper lip when things go wrong; brace up, and let that tree wait a day or so."

But Jamie's sobs broke out afresh. Fireman Jim's head turned languidly away.

"I should think some of those women might know what to do for the boy," said the conductor. The doctor nodded.

"Take him away, and have him amused if you can," said he. "He troubles his father. He ought to have something to eat,"— the doctor hesitated, and then added,— "though I suppose it does no good to say so. Have you anything — any way of making a cup of tea, or any beef extract? Do you go prepared for these emergencies?"

The conductor shook his head.

"I 'm afraid not," he said, "unless some of the passengers might have something left from lunch. We were due at 5:30, you know, and we get our supper in town."

"Well, you might inquire," said the doctor; "he would feel better after having a bit of something."

So the conductor, carrying the crying Jamie, went back to the passenger-car. He found the young girl the center of what seemed almost a social circle.

The good-natured baby, who had been drowsily nodding, was sound asleep in one of the farthest seats, as content as a veteran traveler in a Pullman state-room, while his mother sat shyly on the outskirts of the little company. The traveling-man's sample-cases, covered with a napkin, formed an improvised table; and upon this the stock of eatables was being spread.

"Well, anyhow, we sha'n't be starved," the old lady said; "that there basket"— pointing to a huge covered wicker —"is full of fixin's I was taking to John's folks. I expect it won't seem so like Christmas to the children if they don't have them leaf-cookies and the gingerbread animals; and they *are* good, if I do say it that ought n't; but I 'm sure I never thought, when I was bakin' 'em, that they would save our lives."

"We 'll hope they need not do quite so much for us," laughed the pretty girl, whose name on the one modest trunk in the rear car was "D. M. Marsh"; "but we will not touch the children's cookies unless we are starved into such robbery. How glad I am Aunt Mary made me take this great box of luncheon! I hardly made an impression on it this noon." And she brought out an un-opened jar of pressed chicken. "This will be our Christmas tur-key!" she announced.

"Is n't there some way of melting that down into soup?" asked the conductor, who came in just at this point.

"How is the injured man?" inquired the com-mercial traveler, while the old lady held out her motherly arms for Jamie, as she said:

"You poor lamb! Is it his pa that 's killed?"

"He 's all right," said Conductor Brooks; "only his arm is broken, and he

"JAMIE STOPPED CRYING TO TASTE THE BROTH."

is knocked out and faint. The doctor was asking for some soup, or something to brace him a little. If that was chicken-broth, now, it would just fit."

"Why, we can make broth in just a few minutes," said Miss Marsh; and in a moment she had brought from her trunk a pretty chafing-dish, and lighted it, the old lady nodding approval.

14

"Alcohol, too," the girl said, laughing; "left over from the last oyster-spread at college."

The lamp was quickly adjusted, and into the bright pan went part of the jellied chicken.

"It's a privilege, nowadays, to see a young girl know somethin' about cookin'!" said the old lady, while the stolid-faced man silently proffered a match; and Jamie stopped crying to taste the broth when an appetizing odor began to diffuse through the car.

During all that had passed the boy had hardly left his dark corner. He did not wish to talk. It was nobody's business where he was going, and some one would be sure to ask. But he looked on, and thought how bright and quick and pleasant the girl was. When the broth was sent to Jim, and the doctor returned, the remainder of Aunt Mary's bread-and-butter and pickles was spread, with various additions from the others' lunch-baskets. Part was reserved for breakfast, and the little group whose common misfortune had thawed all reserve supped together merrily if not bountifully. The boy declined all but a single sandwich. He was hungry, but the angry, defiant pride which had hardened his face all day melted somewhat, and he felt less like eating.

"And to-morrow is Christmas!" said the traveling-man, whose name was Osgood. "I've worked like two men to get through and have the day at home with the wife and babies, and it is hard to be stalled up so near."

"And there's my son John and Milly and the children. I have n't missed a Christmas with them since John was married. They all come to me Thanksgivin'," said the old lady. "But we're all alive, and that's a great mercy."

"Never mind," said Miss Marsh; "we'll have the evening at home. But I wish I had n't stayed with Aunt Mary until the last moment."

"I want a Christmas!" sobbed Jamie, his ready tears bursting forth again. "Mama said I should have a Christmas; an' gramma's got a tree, an' I — want — a — Christmas!"

Again the big conductor told the sad little story of the dead mother who had promised a happy day to the boy; and Miss Marsh looked steadily out of the car window a half-minute, while her eye brightened and a resolve formed.

"Jamie boy," said Miss Marsh, "you shall have your Christmas. It's Christmas here just the same as all over the world; and you shall have a real one."

He looked up in joyful trust. "An' a tree?"

"Yes, dear; a real tree," said the girl. The others listened in astonishment. The old lady opened her lips to remonstrate, but shut them again. The traveling-man whistled softly and skeptically, and the doctor looked on amused. Only Jamie and the boy gazed at her with implicit confidence.

"When shall I have it?" asked Jamie.

"To-morrow — Christmas morning," said the girl, brightly. "Now go to papa and go right to sleep, and in the morning — you 'll see!"

With tears undried, but with a face beaming with happiness, Jamie let himself be carried away to his makeshift bed by his father's side.

"An' a tree," he said, as the sleepy eyes closed; "an' candles, an'—"

"WELL?" said Mr. Osgood, with a quizzical smile of doubt. But before Miss Marsh could reply the boy said briefly:

"I 'll get it. I saw 'em before it got dark."

He had already buttoned his coat, and seizing the red-handled ax that hung near the stove, he bravely leaped out into the drifts.

"Those little evergreens, you know," said Miss Marsh; "they are just a few feet away — he can see them by the light from the windows, I think; and we can make it pretty, somehow," she continued eagerly. "Jamie 's such a little lad, and Christmas means so much to him!"

Mr. Osgood nodded.

"But what 's goin' to be on the tree?" asked the practical old lady. "It 's all foolishness goin' to so much trouble for that one child, and we a-tremblin', you may say, between life and death! But I declare for 't, I hate to have the day go by and do nothin'; and even if we 're rescued to-morrow, as that conductor says he thinks probable,— which I don't more 'n half believe,— what with gettin' home, and explainin' when you *do* get there,— which please mercy we may! — why, the day 's as good as gone. An', anyhow, I 've got a pair of red knit mittens for John's Alexander, and I 'm goin' to give 'em to that poor motherless lamb, an' you can hang 'em on the tree for one thing, Miss Marsh."

"Splendid!" said Miss Marsh. "And I have a red skating-cap in my satchel — I believe it will just fit him."

"Is he too small for a knife?" asked Mr. Osgood. "Let 's see — about five, is n't he? My wife makes six the knife-line; I guess I 'd better not," and he returned it to his pocket.

"Hold on!" said he, with sudden inspiration. "I 've some illustrated catalogues here that could pass for picture-books — yes, and cards too — our new ones"; and diving into his cases, he brought out a pile of brilliant pictures.

"Will Miss Santa Claus accept this?" asked Dr. Carleton, offering a

pocket microscope.   Just then the door opened, and the boy came in, dragging triumphantly a small evergreen.

Every one laughed excitedly, and it "did begin to seem somethin' like," as
the old lady said.   Then how they worked!   The tree was braced firmly at
the end of the aisle, the lumps of ice and snow shaken off, and a more durable

CUTTING THE CHRISTMAS-TREE FOR JAMIE.

quality of soft cotton flakes from Dr. Carleton's surgical stores added.
Leaf-cookies and astonishing gingerbread animals dangled from the
branches, and Alexander's red mittens waved in welcome.   Even the man
of the immovable visage helped, with something like a softening of his hard
features ; and when he fastened to a branch a red blank-book and pocket-
pencil, there was an outburst of laughing applause.

Meanwhile Dr. Carleton talked quietly with the shabby little woman.
He had asked about the baby's teething, and she unconsciously gave him
much of her simple story.   Her husband had lost his place in the little town
where they had lived.   He had found work in the city, and she was going

to meet him. They had no " folks." She worked in a factory before she
was married. No; the baby had n't cut any teeth yet She hoped he
would n't fuss or be sick about it, when the teeth came. She did n't know
much about babies.

The doctor listened with sympathy, and a little later, wrapping a bright
gold piece in a bit of paper, he marked it, " For Baby Burns to cut his
teeth on, " and it was added to the tree.

The boy looked on with a dull ache in his throat. He hoped it was not
going to be sore. How sick he had been with those bad throats, and how
good mother always was ! Mother was filling the children's stockings at
home now. She always managed to have something for them, somehow.
Poor mother! She would have it all to bear alone now. How could he
leave her? Why did n't he think of her part? " But I won't go back,"
he said to himself. " I *can't* go back now. I 'll come home rich some day,
and give mother everything she wants; but I won't sneak back now."
Then he did n't care to think more.

" I can make a top," he whispered to Miss Marsh, "if I have a piece of
wood. Shall I ? "

" He would like it best of all, I know," said Miss Marsh, heartily.
Then she added aloud: " Now we must have a star for the top. What can
we do about it ? "

" Well, I guess it 's good enough," said the old lady. " I guess he
won't miss the star."

But the girl looked from one to another in perplexed appeal.

" Why must there be a star? " asked the boy, shyly.

Miss Marsh hesitated a moment. She did not know much about boys,
this brotherless college girl; but she said, almost as shyly as he:

" Don't you think the Christmas star is the most beautiful thing in the
world? You know the Christ Child was born beneath a star; and I think
it meant, for one thing, that for every new life there is a star set in heaven
that will light the life all the way, if once we catch a glimpse of it, and know
it is there for us."

The boy listened breathless. He could not have told just what the girl's
words meant; but the moral courage that all day had been struggling to
live took new strength, and slowly began to shape itself into a resolution.
They stood looking at each other, when the traveling-man, who was down
again in his cases, emerged in triumph, waving some tin-foil.

" Cut out the star from that pasteboard box," he cried ; " and here 's the
glory for it. We can't stop short of perfection in this tree."

" Well, I 'm blessed ! " said Conductor Brooks, staring at the sight,

14*

when he came in a little later. "Where do you folks think you are? At a Sunday-school festival?"

"Never you mind where we be!" said the old lady. Her bonnet was awry, and her spectacles on her forehead. "You just help h'ist up that star, and then we 're all done."

CHRISTMAS morning, Jamie woke round-eyed and expectant.

"I want my tree," he said, "and I want my breakfast." And as the waiting holiday-makers were impatient as he, the breakfast was hurried through, and then they all filed in, Jamie in Conductor Brooks's arms, his father, who was doing bravely, coming behind, followed by the engineer. Jamie gazed at the tree as if dazed by his surprise; but after the first moment, a smile of radiant, ecstatic joy spread over the round baby face. Not a word or sound — only that beaming, blissful smile. It was irresistible; and with shouts of laughter the tree was despoiled of its offerings, and Jamie's cup of happiness was full.

In the midst of the merriment Miss Marsh glanced at the boy. He was gazing at the star with a curious expression, and she thought of their words the night before. In her bodice was thrust a pin whose head was a tiny golden star — the badge of her class society. She drew it out, and pressing it into one of the leaf-cookies which were being passed about, she handed it to him with a whispered "Merry Christmas!" He saw it, and there was a quick rush of color to his face, and tears to his eyes — and that little star weighed down the balance of decision on the right side, and made a man of him. But the girl never knew.

When the laughing talk had quieted a little, Jamie turned confidently to Miss Marsh.

"Now the story," he said.

"What story, laddie?" she asked.

"The Christmas story. Mama said there was a Christmas story, and she saved it up for Christmas day. It is the nicest story I ever heard, mama said."

Every one was still for a moment. Poor Jim turned away. "She would have made a good man of him," was the thought in his heart. The girl felt her own heart beat quickly. Could she? Before all these strange people? What would they think? No, she could n't. She would have a chance to talk to Jamie alone before the day was over. That would be much better. But the childish eyes gazed expectantly into hers, and with a swift thought of the dead mother she lifted the little boy gently to her knee, and with softly flushing cheeks, and voice that trembled a little, she began:

THE CHRISTMAS-TREE IN THE CAR. "THEN THEY ALL FILED IN, JAMIE IN
CONDUCTOR BROOKS'S ARMS."

"Long ago, in a beautiful country over the sea, there were shepherds in the fields keeping watch over their flocks by night."

The sweet voice grew stronger as the simple words of the wonderful story held the listeners in solemn silence. The little woman's tears dropped on her baby's head as she heard of the mother for whom there was no room in the inn, and a vague, trembling prayer went up from her burdened heart to the Christ who was a child.

The boy's eyes shone with new light as he thought of the star set in heaven for the Christ who was a boy, and with a thrill of newly awakened love and appreciation he placed his own weary, hard-worked mother on her throne in her boy's heart.

There were eloquent sermons preached in the churches that Christmas day, and wonderful music was sung; but, as truly as in his visible temples, Christ was preached and worshiped about that little tree, whose balsam breath went up as frankincense and myrrh.

A LITTLE later in the day, after the relief had come and the train pulled into the city station, the Christmas party stopped a moment for the last handshakings and farewells. Twenty-four hours before they would have parted with scarcely a glance at one another. Now they seemed old friends. The busy doctor hurried away first, followed by a long, grateful look from the baby's mother.

" I 'll never forget it of him," she thought.

The boy took a step toward Miss Marsh. One of her hands was tight in Jamie's chubby clasp, the other was held in the old lady's.

He looked a moment, then turned with a resolute face, and walked to the ticket-office.

" Give me a ticket on the first train that goes back to Little Falls," he said.

A Santa Claus Messenger Boy

BY M. M. D.

GOOD-MORROW, my lads and maidens;
Good-morrow, kind people all!
I 'm bidden by dear old Santa Claus
To make you a little call.

And, knowing your gracious courtesy,
I leave you a card to say:
" Remember the little ones of the poor
On the bountiful Christmas day!"

Christmas Eve

BY M. M. D.

ALL night long the pine-trees wait,
Dark heads bowed in solemn state,
Wondering what may be the fate
Of little Norway Spruce.

Little Norway Spruce who stood
Only lately in the wood.
Did they take him for his good —
They who bore him off?

Little Norway Spruce so trim,
Lithe, and free, and strong of limb —
All the pines were proud of him!
Now his place is bare!

All that night the little tree
In the dark stood patiently,
Far away from forest free,
Laden for the morn.

Chained and laden, but intent,
On the pines his thoughts were bent;
They might tell him what it meant,
If he could but go!

Morning came — the children. "See!
Oh, our glorious Christmas-tree!"
Gifts for every one had he;
Then he understood.

www.ingramcontent.com/pod-product-compliance
Lightning Source LLC
Chambersburg PA
CBHW030121030726
47498CB00007B/2496